The Ballad Of Harley Heck

Stuart Bray

All rights reserved Stuart Bray Books 2023

All content featured in this work is property of Stuart Bray Books and Static Books 2023. Violence on the meek Damnation is protected under the United States copyright law. This book is not to be copied or redistributed in any way shape or form without written consent from the author. All characters and situations are fictional and are not meant to resemble anyone or any event. All characters within are sole property of Static books and Stuart Bray. For more information on copyright laws please visit www.UnitedStatescopyrightlaws.gov

Edited by Jason Nickey

Cover by Stuart Bray

Warning: This book contains extremely violent and disturbing content that some readers may find offensive. Readers 18+ recommended.

A NOTE FROM THE AUTHOR

Some of the characters in this story will speak in a distinct dialect specific to the time period and region. If that's an issue for you as a reader/reviewer, you can hop right on YER high horse and fuck right off. I sure as shit AIN'T GONNA give two sucked dicks and a bag of rice. Thank you!

-The guy who writes his books any goddamn way he sees fit.

"Ye haw and fuck you."

Contents

Prologue	1
1. 1869	3
2. Harley Heck	15
3. A Hooker Getting Fucked	27
4. Winchesters and Cum	43
5. Finger Licking	55
6. Hell Has Arrived In Damnation	67
7. Dead Or Alive	83
8. Scum Boys	95
9. Fitted Necktie	105
10. A Goddamned Legend	111
11. Den Of Serpents	121
Acknowledgements	133
About the Author	135
Also By Stuart Bray	137

Prologue

"When I'm good and dead, make sure you pull down my pants and shine my fucking prick."

"Come on now, Harley. Are those really going to be your last words before you face judgement at the feet of God almighty?"

"God? What *God* are you harpin on about, Sheriff? Is it the same God who allowed me to rape, kill, and destroy everything in my path? Is that the God you're referring to? Hell, if so, what's it matter? It's clear as day he doesn't give two shits about you, your family, or this pimple on the Earth's ass that you call a town."

"You seem mighty confident at the moment. I don't think you're going to feel the same way when you're staring up at the hangman's noose."

"Well, I guess I should consider myself lucky. I heard the hangman in this town loved shoving his cock in other men's asses; heard he was a sissy little queer. Son of a bitch might even weep for me once I'm hanging there like a dead cow."

"You sure do have a lot to say for a man who was so hard to track down. How about before I walk you out to the gallows tomorrow morning for all the good folks of this town to watch you breathe your last breath, you do me a favor."

"A favor for a pig? A favor for the pig who's gonna watch me hang? Shit. Why the hell not?"

"Excellent. I've compiled quite the stack of stories told to me by the most vicious outlaws this country has ever seen over the years. I don't think any of them have a story quite like Harley Heck. How about you tell me your story? Hell, you might even become famous someday."

I thought about wrapping my shackles around the sheriff's throat while I watched the life leave his sad old eyes. I would then track down his sweet little family, I would have his wife suck my horse's dick while I fucked his daughter in the brown hole with the barrel of my revolver. Fuck it, I could always do that afterwards.

"Alright, Sheriff. You want to hear my story? I hope you got a fuck ton of that ink, and a lot of fucking paper."

Chapter 1
1869

"*Is it dyin'?*"

"It's '*dying*' you dumb, uneducated fuck." I looked at Rosco as he fiddled with his nappy hair. "You need to learn how to speak proper, or people are going to think you're just some dumb darky."

Rosco was the only colored boy that lived in town. His momma worked over at the general store with Mr. Crawford. All the other kids made fun of Rosco on account of him being colored. I never thought it mattered much; he would be a fucking idiot no matter his color.

"*I been tryin' to talk better, Harley. Momma says I talk good after hangin' out with you some.*"

"Well, I could care less what you learn from me, Rosco. If I have to hear your voice all day, I don't want it to sound retarded." Rosco and I were both about the same age, he had turned ten a few weeks after me. His faded overalls looked as if they were about to jump off his brown skin and into the closest lake.

"Is this horse dying?" Rosco asked properly.

I glanced down at the horse that lay at out bare feet. "He's dying. He'll probably be dead in the next hour. I guess he done slipped off that ledge." I pointed up at the ledge just a few feet in front of us. "That's a good twenty-foot fall. He must've got out of old man Henry's fence."

The dying horse in front of us panted loudly as it tried with all of its strength to lift its head. "We should put it out of it's misery."

Rosco turned to me, putting his hand on my chest.

"I don't think that's for us to figure out, Harley. We should leave it and go tell my momma and Mr. Crawford."

I yanked Rosco's hand from my chest. "Don't put your fucking hands on me, Rosco. You pull shit like that again and you can go back to skipping rocks at the lake by your goddamned self, you hear?"

Rosco lowered his head and took a step back.

"Now that we're on the same page, let's take care of this poor animal." I looked around to make sure none of the construction workers were watching from their camp by the courthouse. "This should do." I picked up a rusty spoon that one of the workers must have thrown in the bushes weeks ago.

"That's just an old spoon, Harley. That ain't gonna work too good."

I rolled my eyes as Rosco turned his head.

"That's a good girl." I said, kneeling next to the mangy brown horse. It neighed loudly. "It's going to be alright. You're on your way to horse hell."

I smiled as I dug the metal spoon into the horse's big round eye. I pushed and pulled until the big round ball popped from its skull.

"Harley, stop!" Rosco grabbed my arm, trying to pull me back away from the animal.

"I told you not to touch me, you fucking piece of trash!"

I headbutted Rosco as hard as I could. He fell on his back as his eyes turned white. "Don't fucking touch me. Don't fucking touch me, Bitch!"

I kneeled back down. The horse neighed louder and louder as I gouged out its other eye. "You poor thing, I hope this doesn't hurt too bad."

I stood up, kicking the horse as hard as I could to the side of its face. The poor animal kicked and tried to roll over, its front legs were too broken to allow it to do so. I kicked it in the face and head over and over again until the strangest sound came from its backside. I walked towards the horse's ass, just about where Rosco was napping. "A baby?" I asked excitedly at the baby horse that rolled around, covered in blood and goo. "You can't even walk yet."

It was sad seeing the poor baby horse without its mother. "How in the world are you going to make it in this awful world without your mother?"

I had to act quickly as I grabbed a red brick from a pile near the worker's camp. I returned to see the newborn foal stumbling around; lost, scared, and confused. I threw the brick as hard as I could, clipping the foal on the side of the head. It fell over to its side, crying out, making the most awful sounding noises. I picked the brick back up, I smashed the baby in the head as hard as I could, knocking it back to the ground. A few more whacks to the side of its head, and it was done for. "I'm sorry it had to be this way."

The foal's head was dented in several spots as it twitched a few more times before finally dying.

I nudged Rosco in the ribs with my foot as the mother horse still blindly kicked and flailed. "Rosco, why did you go and do something like this?" I asked feeling a tad sorry for what I was forced to do next. Those workers must have seen Rosco, and I come back here behind the old courthouse at some point. If they found the dead horse, they would blame us both for killing it. They wouldn't understand that it had to be done. "Excuse me, Sir?" I tugged on the sleeve of a policeman who stood by a lamppost in the center of town.

"What is it?" The policeman asked through a thick gray mustache.

"I saw this colored boy behind the courthouse, he was doing something awful to this poor injured horse!" The policeman knelt down so that he was eye level with me. He seemed almost excited for some strange reason.

"The little negro boy who runs around in those filthy overalls? His momma works over at the general store with that darky lover? Show me, son. Show me now!" The policeman grabbed my wrist, leading me back to where Rosco and I found the horse. I had never seen a child beaten so badly in all my life.

"Harley, tell him it wasn't me!" Rosco pleaded as the policeman kicked and slapped him, ultimately cracking him in the head with a billy club. Rosco's mother was distraught at the sight of her son's body being carried away and thrown into the undertaker's wagon.

"My baby! My baby!" She dropped to her knees and screamed at the top of her lungs as Mr. Crawford did his best to console her.

"Your boy was a sick little creature. Maybe this will be a lesson the next time you let one of your little darky brats run around town acting a fool." The policeman spit at Rosco's mother as she cursed him.

I made my way home through the plains. The dead grass crunched under my feet with each step. I played a thousand scenarios in my mind, none of them worked out in my favor when I walked thought the front door of my parents' cabin.

"Look who decided to come home. Make any money?"

I lowered my head as my father drunkenly approached me, his fists already clenched. I remembered waking up in the middle of the floor while my mother plucked a chicken over the pot in the fireplace.

"Go and get washed up. Don't want your father seeing you filthy before diner."

It felt as if my mother hadn't looked directly at me for over a year. "I'm sorry I didn't make any money today, Momma. I tried selling the pocket watch I took off Mr. Smith last month. The guy by the lumbermill said it wasn't worth squat."

I knew my words would fall on def ears, they always did.

"You should have gone over to the mill; you know those ex-cons want to have sex with anything that has two legs. You could have gone there to make some money, but your selfish mind didn't want to see your ma and pa happy."

I cringed at the thought of going back to the mill. After last time, I swore to never step foot in there again. "I'm sorry, Momma. It hurt really bad the last time. Don't you remember that vet having to sew me back up? It cost all the money I had made that day."

My mother didn't look up at me. I could tell this conversation was over. That night, we ate dinner in silence. Silence from my parents was worse than a kick in the dick by a stubborn mule. Our house was tiny but sat on a large chunk of land that fucking weeds wouldn't even grow on. My pa always made sure to tell me it was my fault that we couldn't farm. If they didn't have to provide for an unwanted bastard, they would have the money for supplies. I laid in the loft above my parents as they fucked. It had become background noise after a while. I wished after they had finished that my father would beat me. I would never admit it to either of them, but I really enjoyed it.

"Lets just leave. Tomorrow night, we grab what we can, we get the fuck out of dodge. That little bastard isn't bringing anything in and I'm sick of staring at dirt and rocks every single fucking day."

Pa had no idea that I was still awake, or maybe he just didn't give a shit either way. They wanted to leave me, they were going to just pack-up and leave me here alone without saying a fucking word. I broke one of my fingers to keep myself awake once I heard the two of them snoring beneath me.

"Ma, Pa, wake up." I whispered standing on the floor next to their comfy bed of straw and cotton. My ma was the first to open her eyes. She screamed once she realized what was happening.

"What in the blue hell!?"

Pa tried to sit up to see what the fuss was about, but the rope around his neck kept him from doing so. I had tied them both to the bed with some old rope I found next to the outhouse. It seemed to work out quite nicely.

"Were you two going to just up and leave me here all alone?"

Ma and Pa turned their heads to look at one another, hoping at least one of them had a good answer that would solve their predicament.

"We was only gonna leave for a few days. Not forever. Do you really think we would just leave a young boy like yourself all alone?"

My Ma's eyes tried desperately to play the role of a caring mother; she just wasn't a very good actress.

"Why did you make me sit in silence at dinner? Why didn't you just beat me like you do any other time? You sick fucks just sat there, not saying a fucking word to me, like I don't exist. I fucking exist!" I screamed in their faces. The look of absolute terror replaced the confusion.

"You don't think we haven't seen you out back touching yourself after punishing you? You're a weird little boy who we can't wait to get the hell away from!"

Damn, they had seen me out by the old barn. They knew I liked it.

"So, you take away the one good thing I have in this world? The one goddamned thing I look forward to. You just take that away?" I had a sneaking suspicion that my parents didn't understand where I was coming from. The pain they had caused by not beating me more.

"Fine, you want us to beat the hell out of you? Untie us and I can promise I will stomp the horseshit out of you! I will beat to fucking death!" My father screamed so loud that the veins in his neck pulsated. I felt that tingling sensation in my trousers. My penis grew hard. I knew if I untied him, he would beat me so badly that I would finally cum. I knew what cumming was, I had just never had the pleasure of doing so yet. It wasn't from a lack of trying. I tried desperately on many occasions to cum. I once drove a nail through my big toe. I grew hard, played with myself, but never came to completion.

"Let us go. Let your pa and I go. Please, Harley."

There were tears in Ma's emerald eyes, unlike my father. I think there was a part of her deep down that cared about me. Stupid bitch.

I lit the extra oil lamp next to the kitchen table. The darkness became flooded with a dim, flickering orange light. In the next few moments, Ma would deeply regret not putting her nightgown back on after getting fucked. I grabbed the iron fire poker that I had sitting in the burning embers of the dwindling fireplace. I smiled at my mother as I felt the heat of the poker as I waved it in front of my face.

"Harley, what are you going to do with that?"

Ma was clearly shaken up. I could tell because she started pissing herself. "Well, Ma, I'm going to hurt you with it. I'm going to hurt you really, really bad."

Her eyes grew larger and larger the closer I came. I honestly didn't think they could get any bigger; that was, until I shoved the pointed end of the poker right up her hairy cunt. To my utter surprise, she didn't scream. "Scream for me, Ma." I shoved the poker further in. The smell of burnt hair made me gag.

"Stop it, stop it now! You little bastard!"

My Pa shouted and screamed at me until he vomited all over Ma's bare-chested tits. Ma's jaw clenched so tightly that her front teeth cracked, and her gums bled. By the time my knuckles were brushing up against her furry beaver, she was dead.

"You little shit! That was your mother!"

"Oh, shut the fuck up, you miserable sack of dick meat."

I pulled the poker out of Ma's gash. A strange popping sound followed as thick chunks of red goo poured out of her now extra-wide hole. "What do you think I should do with you, Pa? Do you regret not beating me harder? I bet you wish you had killed me that day I was robbed in town. I couldn't sit down for a week after that. You always took your frustrations out on me, and though I appreciate it, you're still going to end up as dead as this bitch." I pointed the poker at my lifeless corpse of a mother.

"I do wish I had killed you. You hear me, boy? I shouda killed you fuckin' dead a long time ago! If you're gonna end me, do it now. But just know one thing before you do. Your soul is gonna be as cursed as mine!"

I shoved the tip of the poker into Pa's opened cock deposit. He gagged for a moment before I pushed down with all my weight, sending the poker through the back of his motherfucking head.

"I'd rather my soul be cursed than have my body unbeaten." I threw the oil lamp down on the wood floor, setting the tiny house ablaze within seconds. Before I walked out the door, I made sure to grab Pa's prized Scorpion revolver from the tin box under his bed. I remember being a young boy when Pa returned home from the war with this beauty.

"Took this baby off one of those Yankee faggots after shovin' my rifle up his shitter." Pa said excitedly as he spun the pistol around on his pointer finger like one of the gunslingers I read about.

I couldn't take my eyes off it. The pistol was completely silver with a medium barrel, with cherrywood grips that featured a golden scorpion inlay. "I'm going to kill so many people with you." I kissed the barrel before walking out of the burning cabin.

Chapter 2
Harley Heck

"So, you killed your Ma and Pa? all because they didn't beat you hard enough? Is that what you're telling me, Harley?" The old sheriff looked like he was about to vomit onto the paper he scribbled on. His shaky old hand could barely hold his pencil.

"I wasn't getting what I needed from them, so they had to go. If you don't have anything worth a damn to offer me, I have no need for you."

The sheriff looked up at me, slightly concerned. *"Well, um, I'm telling your story. You'll be famous after this. I promise that."*

I shifted on the bed in my tiny cell. The sheriff jumped back like a cat seeing its shadow. "Easy, Sheriff. Justrepositioning my ass cheeks on this hard as a rock mattress." I laughed.

"So, um," the sheriff scratched his mangy white beard before regripping his pencil. *"What happened next?"* he asked, clearing his throat.

"Well, as I got a little older, I found myself getting bored of strangling prostitutes and reading alone in town libraries. I decided to start a small gang of like-minded individuals."

"You read?"

"Yeah, Sheriff, I read. I've always prided myself on being the most intelligent fella in the room. Not many educated outlaws out there these days."

"Guess all those brains didn't mean much. You wouldn't be sitting in a jail cell waiting to get hanged if they did."

The sheriff's words left a momentary sour taste in my mouth. "You best watch your mouth, Sheriff. The only thing stopping me from smacking those false teeth out of your mouth is some poorly made iron bars."

I read a book once about lockpicking. It's amazing the things you could use to pick a cell door.

"We know all about the poor souls that you've left in your wake. Tell me about the Heck gang. Tell me why you're the only person sitting in a cell, and your brothers in arms are out galivanting God knows where."

I slid my faded gray gambler hat back on my head a bit. My long, greasy hair hadn't seen clean water in a year, give or take. I looked over to admire the wanted poster they had of me up on the bounty board next to the sheriff's crowded desk. "That's one *mean* looking fella on that poster. That thing must've struck some serious fear around this town when it went up."

The sheriff turned in his chair to take another look at the poster for himself. *"The good town of Hope sure was elated when we finally took it down. They called you the devil. Thought you were sent here from hell to cause chaos and destruction. Is that true, Harley? Are you the devil?"*

I looked up as the sunlight from my cell window hit my face. I could hear the sheriff gut his tobacco spit when he got a real good look at my ghostly white left eye, and the deep scar on the side of my cheek that you could fit a coin in. "Do I look like the devil sheriff?" I laughed, flicking my tongue on my rotted black teeth.

"You look like an outlaw that's reached the end of his rope. A lifelong criminal who's about to pay for the sick, twisted things you've done to the innocent people of this sad world."

I leaned back against the red brick wall of my cell, the shadows like a blanket to keep me feeling comfortable. "Guess I'll tell you some more of my story. Don't need you leaving here disappointed."

IT'S BEEN 10 LONG YEARS SINCE HARLEY HECK KILLED HIS MA AND PA IN COLD BLOOD.

"You fellas are makin' this a lot harder than it has to be." I stared down at the two younger looking fellas who were on their knees in front of me. Of course, they were crying and sobbing, begging for their useless fucking lives. It was nothing I hadn't already seen before. Gunner held the boy's lady friend over by the wagon they had rolled up on.

"See anything worth a damn?" I asked out as Gunner threw handfuls of clothes out onto the dirt below.

"Ain't seein' a damn thing worth two shits, Harley."

Gunner was a dumb fuck, and that was putting it lightly. I had found him outside an old church about six years ago, scared and alone with nowhere to go. After I made him suck my dick out back, I knew he was worth keeping around. Now, having my dick sucked by my gang doesn't make me some fairy-ass little queer. If a grown man who's down on his luck is willing to suck your unwashed cock without hesitation, you know he's going to be a loyal little doggy.

"Keep looking. If you don't find anything of value, we'll take the bitch." One of the young fellas tried to be a tough guy after hearing me talk about his little whore in such a crude manor.

"You watch your mouth, you dirty neanderthal!"

I bitch slapped him harder than what my cunt of an aunt used to do to me.

"You want to be a tough guy?" I asked, feeling my blood start to boil. "Sticky." I motioned to the largest member of the gang. "Get this fella undressed for me." Sticky did as he was told, without hesitation.

"Get your hands off of him!" The other boy cried out without attempting to stand up like his buddy just had.

"Don't worry, buddy. I'm not going to lay another finger on your friend here." The still conscious boy looked up at me, his eyes blood-shot from all the crying.

"He ain't my friend, mister, he's my older brother."

I had never smiled with so much satisfaction in my life. I glanced up at Gunner, he knew exactly what I was thinking at that moment. The boys were dressed like they were leaving a church service. I assumed they were a couple of faggots who kept a pretty girl around so folks wouldn't question their sexual preferences.

"Do you realize that you just hit the jackpot?" I asked, sticking my scorpion revolver in the boy's face. "You and your brother here might just make it out of this alive."

Sticky side-eyed me. He wasn't quite privy to my sense of humor just yet. Not like the son of a bitch would ever say anything about it, hadn't heard him mutter a single word in the two-months we've known one another.

"What do we have to do?"

My heart raced with excitement when the younger brother asked those magical words. "Well, I am sure glad you asked. I want you to tug on your big brother's pecker until it gets good and hard. Then, suck on it until he cums down your throat."

"Damn, Harley. That's fucked up."

I turned towards the wagon where Gunner was still perched. "You searched those other trunks yet?" I asked, pointing my revolver in Gunner's direction. His eyes grew the size of a prospector's sifting pan.

"I ain't searched this last one." Gunner pointed down at the truck that was attached to the back of the wagon.

"Well, I suggest you get to it. I don't want to have to go and have Sticky fuck the hole I'm about to put between those goofy looking fucking eyes of yours."

Gunner quickly ran to the back of the wagon.

"Now, back to you." I returned the revolver back towards the younger of the two brothers as the older one started to wake up.

"I don't understand, mister. You want me to do what?"

I kicked dirt into the boy's face after spitting on his chest. "You heard me. Don't make me say it again. Now, tug on that little dick of his." The older brother realized just then what was asked of his younger sibling.

"What the hell is the matter with you? Why would you ask my little-"

My revolver went off, ending the older brother's tirade in the blink of an eye. The look of horror on the face of the younger brother and the girl; it was a moment I would never forget. The older brother's face was unrecognizable now, half of it was missing. "Goddamn, that was a hell of a shot!" I cheered, throwing my hat into the air.

"You- you- Joe! Please, no!"

"Joe? Sounds like a queer ass name to me. Sounds like your brother is better off dead.

Gunner laughed as he finally managed to pop open the trunk. *"Damn good shot, Harley!"*

"Thanks, Gunner. Now, what's in that trunk?" Gunner looked confused as he dug through it.

"Well?" I asked, becoming impatient.

"It's bibles and shit!"

"Bibles?" I asked, not too sure if I had heard the illiterate idiot correctly.

"Yeah, like church bibles."

Gunner held up a black leather-bound bible, a little gold cross on the cover sparkled under the hot desert sun. "The fuck do you faggots have a box full of bibles for?"

I looked angrily towards the younger brother and his little blonde whore that Sticky still had a firm grasp on. "You suit wearing pussies don't have a lick of money on you? But you have a goddamned trunk full of bullshit books!?" I aimed my trusty scorpion revolver just inches from the little prick's chin. "You want God to save you, boy? I am living fucking proof that there is no *God* watching out for a little maggot like you."

"Please, we don't have anything of value. Just let us go and we won't say a word."

The little pussy cried and pleaded for his worthless fucking life. I never understood these fucking maggots. How did they not derive pleasure from punishment? Was that a special trait that only I was lucky enough to possess? I put my gun up to my face, the cold steel felt nice against my sundrenched skin.

"I want you to suck your dead brother's cock. If you don't, I'll fuck the girl." I pointed my pistol at the pretty little blonde bitch that Sticky now had pinned in the dirt like a baby calf. "What's your names?" I asked as I started to undo my leather chaps and unbuckle my belt.

"My name is Lyle. Her name is Judith."

Lyle was shaking like bitterweed in a windstorm. "Okay then, Lyle. Which is it going to be?" I grabbed my crotch as I licked my lips at Judith.

"Take her! Just take her and go. You can do whatever you want with her. She was my brother's wife. She picked him over me."

I peered over at Judith through squinted eyes as the sun came over the valley. "Well, Judith. You're lucky I'm such a gentleman. I believe in ladies first. Now, should I fuck you? Or should I have one of my buddies fuck Lyle?"

Lyle scoffed loudly, then spit in Judith's direction. *"This harlot has no right to decide my fate!"*

I stepped forward and kicked Lyle in the face so hard that my spurs sounded like a bag of coins falling from a tall building. "Shut up, faggot." I laughed as Lyle spit out his front teeth.

"What's it going to be, Judith?" I asked with a wink. Judith looked at Lyle for a moment before turning her pretty face back at me. I couldn't get over how goddamn beautiful this little cunt was. I would end up ripping open her meat-curtains regardless.

"Do what you want with him."

I smiled the biggest smile you had ever seen.

"Please, no!"

Lyle begged for mercy as Gunner rammed his cock in. Sticky held Lyle's arms down in the dirt as Gunner grabbed ahold of his bare-naked thighs. Gunner wasn't a queer, he just liked cumming, didn't matter what in. I watched Judith cry and sob over her dead husband as Lyle was pounded just a few feet away.

"Stop!" His screams echoed through the canyon like an injured coyote.

"I'm taking you with us. You know that, right?" Judith looked up at me, her eyes as green as the water in a horse trough. "I plan on raping you daily, beating you on the hour, until you decide you can't take any more. When that day comes, I'll put you down like a dog in the streets."

Her head dropped into her soft white hands as she screamed.

"Fuck, I'm gonna cum in this fella!" Gunner's head jerked back as he felt his release. Lyle just laid there in the red dirt as blood ran down his legs. He curled up into a ball, still shaking from his life-altering sexual encounter. I sighed as I stood up and walked over to him.

"Just- Just- let me-"

My pistol rang out as I plugged a bullet in the back of his sweaty head. Judith didn't make a peep. "Burn all this bullshit, take their horses."

I holstered my weapon as I watched the thick cum ooze from Lyle's gaping asshole.

"Can we at least give my husband a proper burial?"

"Sure, dig it with your hands."

Chapter 3
A Hooker Getting Fucked

"You made that poor woman dig her dead husband's grave with her bare hands?"

"I'm not some fucking prospector. I don't carry a fucking shovel around. She didn't get very far with the digging anyways. Some of her fingernails came off."

"Why put her through that kind of hell? What did you gain from that?"

"It's simple. Have you ever been to a whore house, Sheriff? Those dumb sluts are so desperate for your money that they'll do anything you want. Even the whores with morals eventually break once you shake them enough. I wanted to shake Judith until she cracked like a child's porcelain doll. She was a strong willed, God fearing, smart woman. She seemed unbreakable. Until she wasn't."

"God almighty. I wish I could take you out back and put you down, right damn now. You're a monster who doesn't belong around normal, good folk."

"Patience is a virtue, Sheriff." I scratched my itchy balls that were sticking to the side of my leg. "You seem to jump the gun an awful lot, now that we're on the subject. I mean, you didn't apprehend me yourself. You sent the best money could buy. You had to go and sick the Murphree brothers on me."

The sheriff shifted in his seat at the sound of the name. "Did you ask them yourself? Or did you have one of your deputies go up the mountain and do it for you?"

"I went myself. I owed it to the people of this world to do anything necessary to catch you. You're lucky to even still be alive after killing one of them. I guess the brothers believe in the law a little more than they're given credit for."

"Maybe those are the same people who believe that the Murphree's are some badass bounty hunting motherfuckers. The Murphree's are a couple of soft-ass faggots."

"That may be, but they did one hell of a job bringing you in."

I couldn't argue with the sheriff who made a valid point. "That's fair. I'm guessing you want to hear about Damnation, and all the trouble I stirred up when I rode in."

The sheriff sat forward in his chair, grabbing his pencil and paper, his eyes fixated on me like someone lost in the desert thinking they found water.

"I want every last detail."

JUST OUTSIDE THE TOWN OF DAMNATION

I planned to send Sticky and Gunner to scope out Damnation while Judith and I hung a few miles back. I found it odd that the dumb bitch never once tried to run away. Must have known how little I needed her, figured she'd take a bullet to the back. We had set up camp the night before. Gunner and Sticky wanted so badly to shove their dicks in Judith's young cunt, but I didn't allow it. Instead, I dragged her into my tent and made her watch me jerk off. Every time she looked away, I would smack her upside the head. The more and more she cried, the faster I stroked. But, like always, I couldn't finish.

"Maybe I need to give you a fucking reason to cry." I said as I smacked her in the face over and over again until she spit blood. I heard Sticky and Gunner giggling outside the tent. They knew about my cum problem. "You two faggots better shut the fuck up!" I smacked Judith a few more times before squeezing her throat until she passed out and threw up all over my canteen.

"You nasty fucking whore." I smacked her at least ten more times before my hand went numb. I poked my head out of the tent, my cock still at full mast. "Head into Damnation. Make sure the law isn't in full force and look out for any marshals. Also, stop by the blacksmiths. I sent him a letter a few months back, he should have something ready for me."

"What do we do if there is marshals and whatnot?" Gunner asked as he sucked down an entire can of baked beans in one gulp.

"Then you come back here and fucking tell me. Is it possible for you to be so goddamn stupid? Did your Ma hold you under water as a youngster?"

Gunner looked up at Sticky, then back at me, the usual confused expression on his face. *"Um, well, not that I can recall, Harley. Why do you ask?"*

I shook my head as I returned to Judith. "You alight, sweetie? I didn't hurt you too bad, did I?" I asked, holding her up with her blonde hair wrapped around my fist. "You want to give it up yet? Have you had enough of old Harley Heck?"

Judith opened her eyes as much as she could considering they were both swollen shut. *"Had enough of what? You can't even cum. What in the hell should I have to be worried about?"*

On a normal day, I would have snapped her fucking neck and tossed her body in the river. But today, I was feeling generous. I ripped Judith's clothes off. I threw her fancy little dress outside the tent for Gunner to sniff at. I pulled out my hunting knife and cut the stings to her corset. "You have some nice little titties."

I squeezed her right nipple as hard as I could. Judith moaned in agony. "This is how you're going to look from now on."

I laughed as I pushed her to the side. Her pale white butt-cheeks pulsated as she rolled. I grabbed a hand full, shoving my pointer finger in her asshole as far as I could get it.

"Stop!" She screamed and then bit down on my bedroll. She knew now that her suffering only made me more excited. I pulled my finger out of her tight hole, then sniffed it like Grandmas homemade apple pie. I became a little overzealous and decided to just bury my face in between those alabaster cheeks. The stench of her unwashed hairy gash kept my dick hard. I shoved my fingers in as far as they could go. "I don't know if I can hold off on fucking you," I whispered into her little pink asshole. Judith buried her face in my bedroll, her hands cuffed together in prayer.

"Our father, who art in heaven, hallowed be thy-"

I shoved my mouth on her cunt, the hair tickled my nose as I shoved my tongue between her meat curtains. "Keep praying!" I punched her thigh as hard as I could, making her gasp in pain.

"*Who's in there?*"

An unfamiliar voice came from outside the tent. It sounded like the voice of an old man. I put my hand over Judith's mouth as she tried to call out. "Who might be asking?" I called out with my hand on the scorpion revolver. I could see the silhouette of a hunched over man carrying what appeared to be a shotgun.

"*You and those other two fellas that just left are trespassing on my land. I advise you to pack it up, and ride on out. I only see this one black horse out here. Are you in there alone?*"

I was becoming annoyed with the old man, especially interrupting such a special moment for Judith. I pulled my revolver, blasting a hole through the tent, the silhouette hit the ground with a thud. I dragged Judith out of the tent by her hair. She screamed and kicked as I slammed her head in the dirt.

"It's alright, Davis." I put my hand on my Hungarian half breed's nose, shushing him softly. "Let's see what we got over here."

I crept around the tent, half expecting the old nut to have his shotgun ready, but that wasn't the case at all. On the ground lay a sad-looking old fool who had taken a bullet to the right of his chest. He was bleeding out slowly.

"I'm sorry. Please, let me go home to my Helen."

I looked down through the plains. A little cabin sat down in the holler, smoke slowly rising from its chimney. "I have to be honest with you, old timer. I don't think you're ever going to see Helen again. Not only because I'm going to kill you good and slow, but because afterward, I plan to head down there to that little cabin and do all sorts of vile things to your Helen."

The old man gasped. He tried to roll to his side, reaching pathetically for his double barrel. *"I won't let some low down outlaws hurt my-"*

I stomped as hard as I could on the old man's arm, snapping it in two. He screamed bloody fucking murder. "Come on now, is that anyway to make a first impression on a new friend?" I asked, kicking the shotgun way out of the mans reach. "I had planned on just killing you so that I could get back to making love to this beautiful piece of fuck meat. But now, I'm going to let my horse fuck you in the ass."

This wasn't the first time I had seen Davis put his giant cock in someone. I found myself in Mexico after running from the law. I had to cross a smelly, shit-filled river to get to a place that smelled more like ass than the river itself.

Found an old saloon out in the middle of nowhere, filled with spics and used up whores.

"You come for the show, amigo?"

"I came for a whiskey and to get out of the fucking desert." I said to the bartender as I slapped a silver dollar down on the piss-covered bar top. "What kind of show could you possibly put on in this shit hole?"

I looked around at the drunk patrons passed out on the floor while ugly prostitutes picked their pockets.

"Oh, you will see. I think you will find it to your liking, amigo."

I rolled my eyes at the fat barkeep wearing his stupid looking sombrero. "I've never seen a saloon that allowed horses inside, especially one as fucking big as that one."

I threw back a shot of some awful tasting brown liquid. "Jesus, I asked for fucking whisky. What the fuck is this shit?" I tossed the glass back at the fat Mexican bartender.

"It's tequila. You don't like?"

I wiped my chin, turning my attention back at the horse in the middle of the room. "No, it tastes like some beaner pissed in it. What the hell is the matter with you people? Is there no class whatsoever in this godforsaken bucket of piss and shit?"

"An outlaw on the run, talking to me about class."

I turned back to the bartender. "What makes you think I'm on the run?"

I knew the answer to his question before he could answer. I just wanted to know how punctilious this spic was.

"You're white, and you're in the ass end of Mexico. That alone says it all. Plus, no offense, señor, but you smell like shit."

The fat jumping bean wasn't wrong. I smelled like a pile of ass on a hot summer day. "So, what are you planning to do with the horse? Do you beat it to death in your show? Some wetbacks give it a hand-job and then drink its thick cum?"

"No, amigo."

The bartender pointed his sausage finger towards the middle of the floor. My eyes followed quickly.

"Dear fucking God!" I couldn't believe what I was seeing. "Is she taking the whole thing?" I asked for the first time in my life while watching a sickly-skinny Mexican girl taking a giant horse cock in the ass. The whore bent down low on her knees underneath the animal. A little Mexican fella grabbed the horse's fat dick, directing it to the proper location. The girl's lifeless eyes rolled back in her head as she moaned loudly. The horse thrusted like a goddamn jackrabbit; its hips thrusted with so much force that the building started to shake.

"That whole thing is inside her, or you're just fucking with me. Which is it?"

Suddenly, there was a commotion.

"Sacarlo!"

The skinny whore's body was being lifted off the ground as the horse reared up. Her arms and legs flopped around maniacally as the huge animal kicked and stomped.

"She's stuck on his cock while she's fucking dead!" I howled in laughter as I gave a standing ovation. I turned to the bartender, a huge smile on my weathered face. "How much for the horse? If I pay extra, can I keep the girl's body attached?"

"This may not even be as bad as you think, Partner." I had buried the old man's head in a small hole I had Judith dig with her mouth. His body kicked and squirmed as I ripped down his rancher pants. "Look at that saggy old ass!"

I laughed as I tried to get Judith to take notice. She looked like she had eaten a bunch of melted chocolate out of a pedophile's bellybutton. "I must say, Judith. You look like absolute shit. Literally. Go wipe your face down by that creek. You're making me sick."

Judith nodded her head like the good little bitch that I was training her to be. "Welp, gotta get to it before you suffocate in there." I directed Davis over to the old mans pale shitter slit. "Get in there, big guy."

I played with Davis's cock for a second before it started flailing around like a wet Billy Bat. The old man's body crumbled as Davis put his weight down on his back. "Get in deep!" I slapped Davis on the backside, he began thrusting harder than I had ever seen. "Fuck, that smells." I backed up when Davis's dick came out by mistake. The old man shot diarrhea out of his ass like a Chinese oilwell. "He must've been backed up."

I shrugged my shoulders as I directed Davis's huge cock back into the old man's pudding maker. I guess it took around five minutes for the old man to either die of suffocation or something in his ass popped. I looked down into the four inch around hole Davis had just made.

"Goddamn, Davis." I said. frowning at the large amounts of cum dripping out onto the dirt. "Guess we better go take care of the old lady. Maybe she knows a trick or two that'll make me squirt this load out." I looked over a small hill where Judith scrubbed her face in the mountain spring water.

"*What-*"

I grabbed the back of her curly blonde hair, then shoved her head under the water. "I know you're the one that's going to make it happen, stop playing these games!" I smacked her now sunburnt ass while keeping my elbow planted on the back of her neck. I grabbed a handful of mud from beside the creek bed. "Let's get you painted up like a chocolate cake." I mashed the thick mud into her pussy and ass crack. I let Judith come up for breath, but only for a moment before shoving her back in the water. My dick was hard behind my pants. I ripped it out so goddamn hard that it hurt.

"You nasty fucking whore!" I shoved it in her pussy, thrusting as fast as I could. The mud made a slopping sound as it pancaked between our thighs. "Make me fucking cum!" I let Judith's head up just to hear her scream.

"I can't. I can't take it any-"

Down her head went once more. The bubbles floated to the top as she screamed underwater. My dick started going soft after just a few minutes. "Fuck! Fuck! Fuck!" I shouted over and over again as I threw Judith to the side, her nude body covered from head to toe in dried mud. "What the fuck is the matter with you, woman? You don't know how to make a man happy? Useless fucking whore!"

I stood up. My limp dick dangled as I kicked Judith in the ass. "Fucking useless!"

I had never been so fucking pissed off in my life. Why couldn't I cum? I had seen those sleazy fucks at the haberdasheries and whore houses do it hundreds of times. Why couldn't I?

"Where are we going?" Judith asked as I tied her hands in front of her.

"We're going to see that fella's wife. Maybe take some supplies and whatnot after I blow her fucking head off." Judith looked so defeated, so sad, so goddamn helpless.

"I don't know why you gotta look so sad for all the damn time. I saved you from a couple of ninnies who wouldn't know what to do with it if you gave it to them." I felt my own insecurities sinking in.

"Why do you do what you do? Why do you need to go to Damnation?"

I tied the other end of the rope to the horn on Davis's saddle. "Hell, we have a little bit of a walk, might as well have some conversation in the air." I tapped my spurs on Davis's side to make him go forward. I hoped Sticky and Gunner were smart enough to stay at camp and not come looking for me if they arrived back before I did.

"I do what I do because I want to. I was never allowed to do anything I wanted to do as a boy. I guess the result of that is a man who doesn't like being told *no*. Plus, I'm doing the world a service, ridding it of the meek, you might say. And as for Damnation... shit, that's just the home of a very fine bank with a very large safe."

I had Davis trout a little faster, making it harder and harder for Judith to keep pace.

"You don't seem like the kind of man who cares about material things. What would you do with the money from that safe?"

Judith's voice was hoarse and raspy. It sounded like she had swallowed a handful of sawdust.

"Wow, you've been with me for such a short time, but you feel that you already know me so well."

I looked back at Judith, her nude body still caked in dried mud, her hair matted down with dirt and grass, her face swollen and beaten. "The boy's care about the money, it was the only way I could convince them to hang around. I suggested that we burn it in the middle of the street after killing as many people as we could. I guess my idea didn't get the majority vote." I chuckled to myself. "Gunner and Sticky are useful to me, for now. Once they wear out their usefulness-"

"You just kill them. Yeah, not hard to tell where that was going. So, you don't care about friends or family. How about yourself? Do you even like who you are?"

I never had anyone ask such invasive questions about my life before. It started to frustrate me. "If people aren't useful to you, why put in the effort to please them or keep them around? It's a huge waste of time and energy that I don't possess. As for myself, I adore who I am and what I've made myself. If I didn't, I would have fed myself a bullet a long time ago."

I yanked the rope hard enough for Judith to faceplant in the tall dead grass. "Maybe conversation in the air wasn't the best of ideas."

Judith quickly pulled herself up before getting dragged across the rough terrain.

"What do I offer? Why are you keeping me around?"

Fuck. Did this bitch ever shut up? I dug my spurs into Davis' side causing him to gallop at a much quicker pace.

"No!" Judith cried out as she smacked the ground so hard that her body bounced before twisting like a Jew's dreidel. We only had a short ride left, I wondered if Judith would survive it.

Chapter 4

Winchesters and Cum

AT THIS POINT IN my story, the sheriff had begun pacing back-and-forth, hands on his hips and all.

"Something the matter, Sheriff?" I asked as I fought back laughter.

"You- you are a sick and twisted monster! How on earth can another human being be so goddamn cruel to another? Especially one as sweet and innocent as Judith Harper? Are you going to tell me at which point in this story you finally decided to kill her? What did you do with her body? Her Ma and Pa have spent the last three weeks looking for her!" The sheriff took a deep breath before sitting back down.

"So many questions mixed with so much emotion, I don't know where to begin." I laughed as I shifted a little on the bed as my ass grew numb once more.

"Begin by telling me what happened to the Mr. Finch's wife. Her body was never recovered from the house you paid a visit to after killing her poor husband."

I thought for a moment, salivating at the memory of the old bitch pleading for her sad life. "I don't think there's enough left of her for you to recover. I mean, unless a piece of jawbone will work for her funeral." I couldn't help but laugh again.

"You think this shit is funny, Harley? You do realize that by this time tomorrow you're gonna be six-foot-under in a pine box, right? There is no stopping that rope from snapping your neck. Death is coming for you, Harley. He rides a pale horse through town the second that noose is tossed above the executioner's head."

The sheriff leaned forward in his chair as he spoke, his eyes burned full of hatred and hellfire as he threatened my life.

"Are you interested in hearing some more of this story? Or are you just going to keep getting all worked up?" I pictured myself lunging forward and grabbing the tired old sheriff by the shirt collar. Twisting his head through the iron bars while tearing off his saggy earlobes.

"Get on with it, Harley." The sheriff picked up his pencil as he wiped the sweat from his brow.

"Now, where were we?"

I climbed off Davis, scratching his neck as I fed him a sugar cube. "You still alive back there?" I looked back at Judith as she lay in the dirt with her hands stretched out in front of her, her body covered in cuts and scrapes. I nudged her head with my boot.

"Hey!" I shouted as she continued laying with her face in the dirt, not making a peep. I pulled my penis from my pants, then proceeded to piss in Judith's hair.

"Excuse me. What are you doing to that poor girl?"

I turned to see an elderly woman with white hair pulled back in a bun. She wore rancher pants that looked almost identical to her husband's, with a stained apron around her waist that was once cotton white.

"Oh, pardon me, Miss. I was just trying to wake her up. I drug her about a mile through the plains, so she might be dead." The old women looked perplexed, not knowing how to respond. "We were just out riding around, enjoying all the nothing that this wasteland has to offer. We saw the smoke coming from your chimney, figured we'd stop by and say hello."

The old woman backed up slowly, her hand reaching around the corner of the front door. "I hope you aren't reaching for a gun. I don't mean you no harm."

The old hag froze. *"Leave the girl behind and be on your way. My husband is due back any minute. He's out hunting."*

I smiled big enough that the old lady could count my teeth from a hundred yards away. "Do you make those pants yourself?" I asked the old lady while nudging Judith with the point of my boot. She looked down at her trousers, once again perplexed.

"Yes, why do you ask?"

"Well, I saw a man wearing those same pants about an hour ago. He was a grumpy old fella with a shotgun." The woman's eyes grew large as realization started setting in. "I had to plug the old fucker with a bullet. Then, I had my horse here, plug his asshole."

The old woman quickly grabbed what she had been reaching for, but not quick enough. I drew my pistol, firing a shot into her left thigh. I knew the bullet went all the way through when I heard glass shatter from inside the house behind her.

"Hell of a good shot." I said, tipping my hat as I walked up the old rickety porch. The old woman rolled around in pain as blood shot from the artery I must have hit. "Sorry about that, blood is such a pain in the ass to get out of wood like this." I holstered my weapon and took a quick peep inside the tiny cabin.

"Take whatever you want. I have some jewelry in the nightstand next to my bed. Just take it and leave."

It was crazy to me how badly the old woman was bleeding; I had never seen so much blood come out of a single bullet wound.

"Now, what in the hell am I going to do with your jewelry? You think I'm here for money, bitch? I'm not here for your useless possessions. I'm here because heading up this way to fuck with you seemed like it would be a lot of fun."

"What did I ever do to you? I haven't hurt you or anyone you love." The old bitch started turning ghostly white as more and more blood drained from the hole I had made.

"Love?" I asked scratching my stubble. "The only thing in this world that I love, the only thing that brings me even a shred of happiness, is watching people like yourself squirm around like the worthless nothings that you are."

I kicked the old woman in between her legs. I felt my heal sink into her mushy old cunt. She let out a gasp, before shitting her pants. "Jesus, what in the fuck?" I asked, covering my nose from the stench. "You're disgusting. No wonder your husband chose to die."

I heard movement from behind me; Judith had woken up.

"Rise and shine, Valentine!" I cheered as I walked down the steps to help Judith to her feet. The front of her body was scratched and bruised so badly that I couldn't even see the coloration of her puffy nipples. "You look like shit ran over twice." I complimented her with a tilt of my hat.

"Who is that?"

Judith pointed towards the dying old lady, not worrying about her own injuries. "We haven't been introduced, but I think the old man said something about his wife's name being *'Helen'* or some shit."

Judith's once young and beautiful face and body looked like she had been trampled by a stampede of angry oxen. *"We need to get her to Damnation. She needs a doctor."*

I walked back up the steps. Helen reached out to me with her wrinkled old hand covered in blood. "What a fucking waste." I rolled my eyes before drawing my pistol once more, blasting a chunk out of the old bitch's face. Her nose and upper lip were missing, and her front teeth were shattered. "Fuck, that's a sight I won't be able to get out of my head." I placed the scorpion revolver back in its holster.

"You didn't have to fucking do that! Why did you have to fucking kill her? Do you feel like a real man for killing a

helpless old lady?" Judith tugged at the rope that kept her from being able to walk more than a couple of feet.

"You're right, she was helpless. The helpless have no place in the west. I did this bitch a favor. Do you think she would survive a winter without a man to hunt for food? She'd be easy pickings for thieves and bandits alike. You should be on your knees thanking me for sparing the old cunt." Judith didn't respond, she just stared at the ground like one of those retards you see in those crazy homes.

"Please, just kill me now." Judith looked up at me through her mangy blonde hair, a tear dripped down her disfigured cheek.

"Kill you? C'mon now, baby. I'm not ready for that just yet."

Judith lifted her head further, her chin almost pointing towards the sky. *"If you're not going to kill me now, just let me go. If you agree to let me, go, I can do something to help you."*

I couldn't help but laugh as I threw Helen's body over my shoulder. "What in the blue hell could you possibly do for me? Please, tell me what a beat-up, useless, naked cum slut can do for someone like me." I tossed Helen's body down the well next to the house. I heard her body smack the stone wall on its way down into the darkness.

"I'll make you cum."

I turned to Judith, one eyebrow raised, and my interest piqued. "How do you figure you're going to do that? I already fucked you; didn't anything happen. Do you have some secret slit hiding underneath your little pink shitter that you aren't telling me about?" I looked behind her, smacking her thick ass with the palm of my hand. Judith cringed in pain as I watched my handprint fade into her sunburn.

"Death and pain get you going. I've learned that the hardest of ways. How about we do something to really get you going?"

Judith lifted up her hands, motioning to the ropes around her bruised wrists. I pulled my knife and cut them with a single swipe. She grabbed my hand softly as she led me up the porch and into the cabin. I put my hand on my pistol as Judith grabbed a Winchester repeater that sat next to the door.

"Its okay." Judith whispered as she handed me the repeater. She climbed up onto the old couple's dining table, lying flat on her back with her legs spread open. Her pussy was pink and slightly swollen. She spit in the palm of her hand, then used the spit to wet her gash.

"This is supposed to get me to cum? You like wasting my time, bitch?"

Judith smiled as she pointed to the barrel of the repeater. *"Tug on your penis while you fuck me with that."*

I became hard before she could finish spewing her request. I wasted little time in pulling out my cock and shoving a few inches of the barrel into Judith's used cunt. She winced in pain, so I started stroking. "Does that shit hurt?" I asked with a bead of sweat dripping from my brow.

"Yes." Judith closed her eyes tightly, biting her bottom lip.

"You look like a fucking whore!" I stroked harder. Before I knew it, half of the barrel was inside Judith, I pulled it back and forth aggressively. I noticed blood dripping from the sides of her hole. "You worthless cunt of a whore!" I growled as I rammed the repeater in as far as I could.

"Stop!" Judith screamed as she grabbed the barrel, trying to force it out of her. The sheer look of agony on her face made my nut sack tingle.

"Fuck!" I called out as I shot a hot load of cum all over Judith's thigh. "I fucking came!" I dropped to my knees. The ecstasy that I felt in that very moment was impossible to put into words. It had finally happened. After all these years of trying to shoot this load, I had fucking done it. The sound of a lever action repeater being cocked brought me back to reality.

"Don't fucking move. I will not hesitate to put a hole through the center of your ugly fucking forehead!"

Judith was standing atop the dining table, the barrel of the repeater now aimed down at me.

"You wanna kill me, bitch? You think you have what it takes to be a killer?" I could see the scared little girl behind those fiery green eyes. "Well, go on. Shoot me."

I pulled my hat off, tossing it to the side. "You know what would be funny?" I asked as I pushed back my long hair. "How bad of luck would you consider it if that weapon wasn't loaded?" I asked with a devious grin. Judith hesitated for a moment as she turned the gun to the side, checking the chamber.

"Urgh!" Judith let out a very unattractive grunt as I kicked the right leg of the wooden table, sending her headfirst to the floor below.

"You stupid bitch." I would have bet my life that her neck was broken. She landed on the top of her head so violently that her chin touched the center of her little titties. The only obvious reason I knew she hadn't died from the fall was the fact that she was now trying to get to her feet and run towards the open front door. "Where you running off to?"

I got to my feet, tucking my cock back in my pants. Before she could make it to the bottom step, I threw my pistol at the back of her head as hard as I could. It made a loud cracking sound as it bounced off a spot behind her ear. Judith fell to the dirt with a thud.

The old woman had some clothes in a trunk at the foot of her bed, I slid them on Judith's unconscious body before tossing her on Davis's back. "Let's see you run now, baby." I slapped Judith on the face with everything I had in me.

Chapter 5
Finger Licking

"How did you keep a young, naked woman around two other degenerates like yourself without causing a rift in the group?" The sheriff wiped his face with a handkerchief. He started to look sickly after hearing the part about shoving the gun barrel in Judith's pussy hole.

"I told them that she was my property. They could either respect that, or I would just kill them both like dogs. Gunner and Sticky knew better than to test me."

The sheriff turned the page of his little notepad. *"Big words coming from a murdering rapist who's sitting behind bars, just waiting to hanged."*

There it was again, the sheriff kept finding these opportunities to take a jab at my reputation and livelihood. "Do tell me something, Sheriff. How much shit would pour from your wrinkled old asshole if I was to stand up and walk straight through these bars and wrap my hands around that turkey pussy of a neck?"

The sheriff gulped loudly as he grabbed another pinch of chewing tobacco. *"I guess it wouldn't matter much. If you somehow escaped, the Murphree's would find you once more, drag you back here, and you would still face justice."*

The worn-out old sheriff tried to play tough guy; it didn't suit him.

"Aw, yes. The Murphree brothers." I tapped my pointer finger on my knee. The thought of those hillbilly fucks dragging me back to Mommy and Daddy like a pouty child pissed me off.

"Shall I fucking continue, sheriff?" I asked, just imagining myself strangling this smug prick. The sheriff pulled his silver watch from his coat pocket. It swung back and forth from a small chain.

"I might have time to hear a little more. It'll be sundown in an hour, give-or-take. The wife is making shrimp gumbo tonight. Don't want to be late that."

He rubbed his stomach, as if to torment me further.

I returned to camp with Judith still out cold on Davis' back. Sticky and Gunner sat next to a dwindling campfire. "Tell me something good." I demanded as I unmounted

Davis and walked him over to a crudely made hitching post. Sticky and Gunner looked at one another before turning back to me with fear in their eyes.

"Well, Harley. Um, there isn't much good to tell." Gunner replied shakily.

"Damn, Gunner. It's about to really suck to be you." I pulled out the scorpion revolver, aiming it in Gunner's direction. Sticky quickly moved out of the way.

"It ain't my fault, Harley. There's a bunch of them lawmen down there, a few Marshalls too. They armed to the tooth, I tell ya. I's sorry I ain't got any good news to tell of." Gunner held up his hands to shield his mousey looking face.

"Put your hands in the fire until you can tell me some good news."

Gunner's mouth dropped open as he looked over at Sticky for help. "Don't look at him, you little rodent. Stick your goddamn hands in that fire or I'm going to blast you a new asshole."

I pulled the hammer back. Gunner stuck his hands into the hot embers under the burning logs. "Good boy. Now, don't be taking them out until you can tell me something that's going to make me really happy to see the two of you." Gunner's face turned red, sweat poured down his face like a wet washcloth being rung out.

"It hurts, it hurts so bad, Harley. Please, let me take them out!" Gunner's high-pitched voice went up a pitch higher.

"Tell me something good. That's all I need." I said as I sat down on the log next to him. I could already smell the cooking flesh from his fingers as they sizzled loudly.

"Fuck, Fuck! Please!" Gunner's screams were so deafening that I had to scoot over a few inches.

I leaned over to scream in his ear as he cried like a little bitch. "Make me happy!"

"The bank. The bank is havin' work done on it. It's closed to the public for the next week!"

I grabbed the back of Gunner's vest, yanking him off the log and onto his back. He held his charred hands out in front of him. He screamed and screamed until I kicked him in the side of the head, putting him to sleep for the time being.

"How long has it been since we've had cooked meat?" I asked Sticky as he watched me use my knife to cut off Gunner's left thumb. The meat was overdone, but not terribly awful. "Get out your knife and get you a couple for yourself." I motioned to Sticky as he fought back vomit. "You fellas need to start appreciating all I do for you. I'm getting sick of the disrespectful looks, questioning my methods, and the bad fucking news!"

Sticky just sat there with a far away look in his eyes. Sticky wasn't nearly as ugly as Gunner, but he wasn't getting discounts at the whore houses or anything like that. I had wondered for the longest time why Sticky never spoke. One night when he was fast asleep, I realized there wasn't a tongue in his mouth. It took everything in me to not sick my dick in to see what it felt like. I ended up trying it out on some little colored whore in Jackson. The madam of the house didn't take very kindly to me cutting out one of her workers tongues, then forcing her to finish waxing my pole. I ended up having to kill eight or nine of those bitches before I could be on my way. The papers called it 'The whorehouse massacre'. I always *kinda* liked that headline. "Guess the bitch has got to eat." I rolled my eyes, cutting off one of Gunners pinkies.

"I bet Gunner is going to be confused as hell when he wakes up and has to scratch his balls with a stump." I laughed hysterically while Sticky stared up at the night sky.

"I've always wondered how you lost your tongue." Sticky looked down at me, the flames flickered in his dark brown eyes. Every scar on his face like white slashes from an angry cougar. "You want to know what I think?" I tossed the picked clean finger bone into the fire pit. "I think you were a rat. I think your tongue being cut out was a way to teach you a lesson." I waited for any type of response from Sticky, but he just sat there staring through me like I wasn't even there.

"You've been quite helpful to me, more so than this fucking idiot." I nudged Gunner with the heel of my boot. "Good help is hard to come by these days. All the outlaws are trading in their guns for a pipe wrench and a timecard. This world doesn't tolerate our kind anymore. We're a dying breed."

Sticky nodded his head to show that he agreed.

"Can you believe I once ran the biggest gang this side of the river? I had almost twenty guns strong at one point. Most of them died fighting the good fight. The rest, I trapped in a cave a few years back. Guess they never found a way to dig themselves out."

Sticky's eyes grew slightly large after hearing what had happened to those before him.

"Don't look so surprised, Sticky. Two of the whores we kept around ended up pregnant cause a few of the boys didn't know how to pull out. You can't lose focus in this line of work. A couple screaming babies would have turned my gang into a goddamned laughingstock. I couldn't have that. I brought the whores down to the deepest part of the cave we were hiding out in. I shot them in their bellies and left them there to bleed out. I guess the rest of the gang thought my actions were a bit cruel. They all ran down there to save the whores and the bastards they carried in their infested wombs. I walked out after planting a stick of dynamite at the exit. I blew that fucker up, sealed those traitors inside their tomb to rot."

Movement beside me meant that Gunner was waking up. *"My- my- my fingers! Where are my fingers?!"*

I rolled my eyes at Gunner's overly dramatic tantrum. "Oh, would you please shut the fuck up?" I asked as I started feeling a tad irritated thar my story had been so rudely interrupted. "I was in the middle of spilling my guts out to Sticky. Somehow you had to go and make it all about you." I shook my head at Sticky, who looked concerned for his retarded friend.

"My fingers done fell off, Harley. You burnt 'em to a crisp in that fire!" Gunner held his hands up to my face, only four fingers on his right hand remained.

"Calm down, they didn't burn off in the fire. I cut the damn things off and ate them while you were on the ground sleeping like a lazy piece of shit."

Gunner began gagging loudly. He vomited all over the log we had both been sitting on at one point. "You are one nasty little fucker, you know that?" I asked, laughing as I scooped up chunks of puke and threw them at Judith, hoping it might wake her.

"How am I supposed to shoot? I ain't got no fingers to hold my pistol!"

For the first time in his life, Gunner made a good point. "You know something, Gunner? I think you might be even more useful now. How about you walk into that bank with a few lit sticks of dynamite strapped to your chest. That way, Sticky and I don't have to worry about blowing the safe."

Gunner looked up at me, his eyes full of dread and confusion.

"I would die, Harley. I would get blow'd up durin' the explosion. How could I spend that money if I'm in a million pieces?"

I looked at Gunner, then at Sticky, then back at Gunner once more. "I guess you got yourself a good point there, Gunner. I guess you wouldn't be spending any of that money because you would be dead as fuck. But, you see, you can't shoot a gun. That means that you're essentially worthless to me. You going in there with that dynamite would make you worth something to the gang, it would make you worth something to me." I put my hand over where I assumed my heart was. Gunner looked over at Sticky, hoping he would do something to change my mind. Sticky took a deep breath and lowered his head.

"*I don't want to die, Harley. Please, don't make me do that.*"

Sticky shifted his weight on the log where he had been seated. I could tell he had a soft spot for Gunner. "Do you want to fuck him?" I grabbed the back of Gunners neck as I smiled at Sticky. "Do you want to put your dick inside this little rat fucker? I always took you for a big ole faggot. Guess I was right."

Sticky's facial expression changed dramatically after my insinuation. "How about this. Since you two are so in love with each other and could give a fuck-less about me or this gang, you should kiss." I shoved Gunner forward, almost landing him in the hot ash of the firepit. "Kiss this rodent on the fucking lips, or I blow his fucking skull apart!" I pulled out the scorpion revolver, aiming it at the back of Gunner's head as he sobbed like a scared child. Sticky stood up and placed his hand on his old Colt. I clicked the hammer back on the scorpion revolver. "Fucking try it, Sticky. Just fucking try. I'll end this little fuck before you take your next breath." Sticky slowly removed his hand from the pistol, his eyes wide like a cornered rabbit.

"*Where are we?*" Judith's voice broke the awkward silence. She pushed herself up from the dirt. I smiled watching her struggle.

"We are right in the middle of a very saucy predicament." I winked at Sticky as he began to sit back down.

"How did I get dressed? Whose clothes am I wearing?" Judith studied her outfit through her swollen eyes. I must have knocked her out pretty darn good.

"They belonged to the old whore we visited a few hours ago. You don't remember?" I was honestly a bit disappointed that Judith didn't recall the fun we had today. What fun is suffering when you're not capable of remembering it?

"I remember an old man and your horse, nothing after that."

I clenched my fists. I had never felt so angry in my entire fucking life. "You don't remember the gun in your pussy? You don't remember watching that old bitch die on that porch? You don't even remember what I- um- what I did?" I thought back to the explosion of cum that I painted the old lady's kitchen with. My dick started tingling against my thigh.

Judith looked up in horror at the three of us. I hoped it was all coming back to her. *"How could you do such awful things to someone who has never committed a sin against you? What did I do to deserve the atrocities you've committed against me?"*

Sticky and Gunner looked like two deer who were just shined with a lantern during the darkest night in the woods. I rolled my fucking eyes; I was never one for dramatics.

"You and your faggot friends took the wrong goddamn turn out there in the desert. If you had just kept going straight through to Ned's landing, your fucking wagon would have never come our way. I've done and will continue to do whatever the hell I please to you, bitch. Your ass, your pretty cunt, your fucking soul, belongs to Harley fucking Heck."

Gunner started whining again about his fingers, making what I said look inconsequential and forgettable. *"I'm in a world of hurt right now, Harley. I don't think I can take it much longer. I need a doctor or sumthin'."*

I pulled my pistol, placing the tip of the barrel under Gunner's chin meat. "Shut the fuck up. I shouldn't be doing this for you, considering you've been a pain in my ass tonight, but I am a forgive and forget kind of fella."

A small glimmer of hope twinkled in Gunner's eyes. "Instead of giving your boyfriend over there a kiss, I want you to shove that crispy nub of yours in his ass."

Gunner looked over at Sticky, the glimmer of hope faded quickly. "If I have to wait any longer, or I have to tell you a second time, I'll kill you both." Sticky stood up, unbuckled his sheepskin chaps, and dropped his pants. He knew how serious I was.

"Get over there, Gunner. Shove that crispy little nub as far up his shitter hole as you can get it." Sticky's face went ghostly white as he bent over like a bitch in heat. "You better be inside that ass before I reach the count of five." I tapped the tip of my scorpion revolver on the top of Gunner's head. "One, two-"

"I'm goin'!"

Gunner jumped to his feet and ran over to his bent over friend. Sticky's ass was covered in thick black hair, little dingleberries hung from his chafed crack. "Get it nice and wet, you got a lot of shit to get through." I watched as Gunner stuck what was left of his mangled hand into his mouth, saliva dripped from it as he positioned the nub to go up Sticky's unwashed turd cutter. Judith vomited out what little was left in her stomach as she watched on in absolute shock and disgust.

As dawn came forth, we readied ourselves for the bank robbery. It was bound to be one hell of a day.

Chapter 6

Hell Has Arrived In Damnation

"I'M GOING TO LOOK past the bizarre shit that you did leading up to the bank robbery. There is no way in hell that I can put into words how twisted and evil of a person you have to be to make people that trusted you with their lives do something so heinous to one another. I want to hear about the bank. Tell me how you managed to make it out of the vault with your head still attached."

The sheriff stood up to pace back and forth like had done many times since. "You call me evil, but that couldn't be further from the truth. I am what I am, an outlaw. I stayed true to what I was. I never strayed off the path. I was never anything less. If you choose to live this life, you are well aware that it will be a short one."

The sheriff picked up his big white hat, placing it on his balding head. His badge needed a good cleaning; it didn't shine the way it was supposed to. "You plan on retiring soon? Your badge is all smudged up and you don't keep your pistols loaded. You must have been growing quite bored before my arrival."

The sheriff looked down at his badge before spit shining it rather quickly. *"Don't have no need to keep my guns loaded in this town. We don't see trouble the likes of you very often. I haven't had to point this weapon at anyone in over ten years."*

I laughed to myself as the decrepit old sheriff sat back down in his chair in front of my cell. "Must be why this town wants to see me hang so badly. They act like I'm some kind of parasite feasting on their happy little lives. I bet I won't be buried in that cute little cemetery up on the hill. I'll be burned or tossed in a cart of cow shit, taken off to be dumped in some asshole's garden."

It seemed like it was the sheriff's turn to get a good laugh of his own. *"Hell, Harley. Even that wouldn't be good enough for the likes of a famous outlaw like you. We plan on sticking you in a cheap pine box with about a hundred pounds of chain wrapped around it, just in case your corpse decides to rise up from the grave. Then we're going to ride that sucker out to the swamps and dump it in the most foul-smelling hole we can find."*

I had never felt so honored in my life. "Gee, Sheriff, you really know how to make someone feel special. Maybe I'll get lucky and catch cholera while I'm in here drinking this nasty fucking water. Maybe I'll shit myself to death before I ever get a rope around my neck."

"Am I supposed to just sit here while you go out on your suicide mission?" Judith asked as I strapped my last few sticks of dynamite to Gunner's chest.

"You'd love that, wouldn't you? It would give you enough time to undo those ropes and get the fuck out of dodge. But no, you're actually joining us."

Judith looked up at me, but oddly, she didn't seem disappointed, or even frightened.

"What do I get to do?"

I glanced up at Gunner as he stared into the cloudless blue sky. "You're going to be my insurance. Your job is to have my pistol pressed up against your temple while I make demands to the folks who survive the blast."

"The hell with that!"

I turned in complete surprise. "What should I have you do, then?" I found myself curious for the first time in a long while. "Should I trust you standing behind me with a loaded gun?" I laughed, then made sure to tie the fuse to Gunner's shit smelling nub. "Make sure you light this bad boy before you make it through the front door, don't give any of those fuckers a chance to take cover." I put a match in Gunner's 'better' hand. "You hear me, boy?" I asked slapping him in the face so hard that his eyes went in different directions.

"I want something to do! I'm not going to be some damsel in distress that you do with what you please."

I turned to give Judith my full attention. "I've been doing what I please with you for the past two days. Why should things change all of the sudden?"

Judith looked up at me from the ground where she lay tied up, her eyes burning with anticipation. *"If this is my situation, and these are my final days, I want to do something daring. I've never been the audacious type. I need to prove to myself that I am more than some church going housewife."*

I thought for a moment how funny it would be to watch Judith's body twitch after being pumped full of bullets once the police showed up. I laughed out loud before kicking her in the stomach so many times that she coughed up a nice puddle of blood into the dirt. "How's that for daring?" I asked, spitting on her as she moaned in pain.

I caught Sticky shaking his head at me from the corner of my eye. "Something you want to get off your chest, Sticky?"

His disapproving expression never faded. He and I both knew that he wouldn't survive this robbery. He knew that he wouldn't see a single cent from the inside of that bank vault. "I bet you think I'm going to shoot you in the back of the head once we make it through those doors, don't you?"

Sticky nodded.

"I have to say, Sticky. This tension between the two of us has to stop. I'm so goddamn sorry that I ate Gunner's fingers. I'm sorry I had him fuck you in the ass with his nub. I'm sorry I haven't been sensitive to your feelings." I put both hands on my chest as I pouted my lower lip. "Can you find it in your heart to forgive me?" I asked, trying my hardest to sound sincere.

I guess Sticky wasn't buying it. He just stared at me without blinking. "Come on, Sticky." I extended my arms for a hug. Sticky shook his head defiantly.

"You fucking coward."

I turned to Judith who had finally stopped coughing up blood and stomach acid. "What was that, you little cunt?" I asked with a smile.

"You must be as deaf as you are a fucking pussy."

Judith Propped herself up. The dried blood oh her lips looked like the lipstick that whores wore in the saloons. "Keep going, Judith. Tell me more about myself." I sat down on the ground, I placed my arm around her lower back, my hand grasping tightly on her left breast.

"You bully people around with your gun. It's the only thing that gives you any power. Without that weapon on your hip, you're nothing but a scared, defenseless, fucking coward."

I used the tip of my finger to play with Judith's rock-hard nipple.

"Gotcha!"

I drew the scorpion revolver just as Sticky reached for his sidearm. The shot sounded like a sharp bolt of lightning splitting a tree in half. Sticky dropped to the ground; smoke poured from the little black hole in his chest. "Too slow, you fucking traitor." I spit on his body as he bled out like a stuck whore. Gunner screamed at the top of his lungs as he ran to Sticky's side.

"You're okay. It'll be alright!" Gunner held Sticky's head in his arms as he cried.

"Well, looks like its just me and you." I laughed as I holstered my weapon. "Did you get what I asked for from the blacksmith?" I asked, nudging Gunner with the tip of my boot. He looked up at me with snot running down his nose and his eyes full of tears.

"It's in the bag on my horse."

I thanked Gunner as I pulled the heavy sack from his horse. I had sent a letter to the blacksmith in Damnation a few months back using a false name. I had read something about the Australians wearing suits of armor made from steel scrap. I pulled the helmet from the sack. It looked quite crude, but very effective. I pulled the helmet over my head, it fit like a big steel bucket. There was a small rectangular slit I could see from.

"Jesus, this fucker will cook you like pork pie if you keep it on too long." I laughed as I tossed the helmet to the side, grabbing the thick chest plate that came with it. The steel matched the helmet, a blackened steel that looked as if it had been tempered on the surface of the sun. "What's this?" I felt something else in the bag. I was surprised with a pair of armor-plated gloves. "Well, thank you Mr. Blacksmith. Hope you don't plan on withdrawing any money today." I chuckled as I watched Gunner get to his feet.

"How could you, Harley? How could you do that to Sticky? He was loyal to you, just like me. I'm not doing this robbery. It's not worth it anymore. I'll keep my mouth shut. You don't have to worry about that."

The fear in Gunner's voice was as obvious as an elephant in an outhouse. I grabbed Gunner by the throat, squeezing the tips of my fingers in as hard as I could. "You're right, Gunner. You have been a loyal little mutt, but your faggot friend had it coming. Do you really believe that I would let you just walk away? You must really be as dumb as you look."

I used my free hand to reach into Gunner's cesspool of a mouth. I grabbed his two front teeth between my pointer finger and thumb, I snapped them in half with little effort.

"Urgh!" Gunner cried out in distress. I tossed his broken teeth into what was left of the fire.

"You're going in that fucking bank, you're going to light that fucking fuse, you're going to-"

My tirade was cut short when what I assumed was a rock cracked me in the back of my head. I fell to my knees as little blue and red spots danced around on the ground like big-top performers at the circus.

"You sick bastard!"

The last thing I heard was Judith's voice as I was struck in the head once more. Only this time, the lights went out. I came to with a pounding headache and the sensation of dried blood sticking to the back of my neck.

"Goddamn." I grunted as I pushed myself out of the dirt. The dead grass that stretched for miles across the plains was all I could see. "Where?" I turned to see camp just a few yards to the left. Gunner sat on a log, stoking the now roaring fire. I stumbled over towards him, my head pounded like a Cherokee drum. "What in the fuck was that?" I asked, still trying to regain my composure.

"The lady got free. She hit you with that rock over there."

Gunner pointed to a rather thick rock covered in my blood. "Where is she? and where is Sticky's corpse?" I asked when I realized Judith was nowhere to be seen and all that was left of Sticky was a puddle of blood where his body had been lying.

"After she hit you with that rock, I choked her until she went to sleep. I took Sticky's body down to the river. He woulda liked that. I put the lady in your tent. She's been out for an hour, give or take."

The smell of baked beans came from the pot that hung over the fire. "How did I end up all the way over there?" I asked pointing to where I had woken up. Gunner looked over at the spot, then back at the fire. He didn't seem like the same person he had been just an hour before. This wasn't one of those times where he pouted like a grown retard. Gunner seemed defeated in some way.

"Your ass still chapped about Sticky?" I asked sitting next to him on the log. I could see Judith's feet sticking out of my tent. I wondered if she was dead. Gunner had moments where his inner retard would break through, it was like watching a human muskrat that didn't know its own strength as it punched and broke shit.

"I moved you cause the fire was real hot once I got it goin. I ain't mad about Sticky no more. I told you I was loyal. I hope you believe me now."

I hated to admit it, but I was proud of Gunner. "Goddamn, boy. I'm impressed. Now, let's get ready to rob this bank. You have some dying to do today." Gunner looked at me like he was surprised that I hadn't changed my mind about his role in today's festivities.

"You still want me to do that, Harley?" Gunner reached up to touch the dynamite still attached to his chest.

"Well of course I do, you fucking retard. I told you that you were useless with your hands like that. Did you think I was going to change my mind just because you decided to be my little bitch one last time?" Gunner looked like a sad puppy, a sad puppy that I wanted so badly to stomp on.

"I just don't wanna die, Harley. What if I could get married one day? I could have some youngin's of my own. I'm only twenty-eight years old. I got my whole life ahead of me."

I laughed as I slapped my hand down on Gunner's back. "The thought of a creature like you reproducing makes me want to fucking gag. What makes you think any woman that you aren't slipping a dollar bill to would ever want your ratty little cock in them? Let alone pop out your ugly ass spawn."

Gunner looked down at his boots. I could tell he was going to start pouting again. "I'm going to get my armor on. I want you saddled up by the time I'm done." I gave Gunner one more pat on the back before preparing for battle.

"What- what happened?" Judith poked her head from the tent. Her eyes widened at the sight of me in my armor.

"How would you like to kill some people?" I asked, my voice echoing inside the steel helmet. Judith looked confused. Bruises covered her neck where Gunner had choked her out. "I'll look past the hitting me with a rock incident. I'll chalk it up as womanly vapors." My voice sounded so ominous that it sent a slight chill up my sweaty backside. I did really plan on looking past Judith's unpardonable sin. I would get what I needed before twisting her head from her measly body.

"If I help you, will you let me go afterwards?" Judith sounded like she had been gargling nails. It must have been excruciating just trying to speak. I knew she wouldn't like my answer, but what choice did she have in the matter?

"No. If you don't die during, I'll just kill you after."

Judith reluctantly nodded. It was at that moment I began to realize that Judith was becoming less afraid of death. "Gunner, get going ahead of us. Remember to light the fuse before you're through the door. Get as close to the vault as you can. That way it saves me the trouble of having to plant the dynamite myself."

Gunner looked up at me as I mounted Davis. *"Please, please, Harley. Please don't make me do this, I'm beggin' ya."*

I smiled at Gunner, then tipped my hat at him. "See you in hell, buddy."

I turned Davis so that his head pushed Gunner forward. Gunner let out an ear-piercing screech. "At least die with some dignity for fucks sake." I rolled my eyes as I continued to use Davis to push Gunner forward. "You do this right, and I'll make sure I send your cut of the money to your Ma." Gunner stopped, then turned to look up at me once more.

"You mean that, Harley? You really gonna send my momma my cut?" There was that flicker of hope in his eyes that I had seen earlier.

"You have my word." I extended my hand for a shake. Gunner forced a smile and returned the favor. After making our way down the hill, Gunner in front, Judith riding Sticky's horse in the back, it was time to raise hell. "Get on in there." I pulled my gun and aimed towards the bank. Gunner looked up at me one last time before running towards the front door. This end of town still had dirt roads, unlike the other end with its cobblestone streets.

There was no sign of any workers near the bank, nor any lawman out patrolling the area. This end of town was being renovated now that Damnation had a new mayor, a man who preached about a better, brighter future that would ultimately never happen.

"When that dynamite goes off, people are going to wonder what's going on. You're not going to have much time."

I turned to look at Judith who was, all of the sudden, a professional bank robber. "Shut your mouth, bitch. This isn't my first rodeo, won't be my fucking last either." My voice sounded deep and demanding under the steel helmet.

Judith looked at me like I had just pissed on her beaten-up face. A part of me believed that Judith wasn't as afraid because she thought I would have a change of heart, maybe fall in love with her like all the boys did when she was sitting pretty in the schoolhouse. In reality, she was my backup armor if the set I was wearing failed. Would the law shoot a helpless woman? I guess it was time to find out.

"He's in!" Judith cried out as soon as Gunner pushed the double doors open. A few seconds later, there was an explosion that made every window in the small building shatter outwards in a hailstorm of glass and debris.

I tossed Judith the old man's shotgun. She looked at it for a moment before glaring up at me. "You even think about aiming that gun in my direction, I'll put you down before you even realize there's a big hole between your eyes. You understand, bitch?" Judith nodded like the good little cunt she had become.

"You got two shots, make them count." We raced towards the opened front doors, dismounting before even reaching the steps. Clouds of dust and smoke poured from the broken windows. The main lobby covered in thick chunks of Gunner. I looked around for a vault, but only saw a dark green safe sitting in the far corner of the room.

"There's no fucking vault. This fucking bank still uses a goddamn safe!" I guess Gunner had gotten close enough to the safe that it caused quite a bit of damage. "Put your arm in there, pull out everything you can reach." I pointed my gun towards the jagged hole under the thick steel door.

"I'll try."

"No trying, just fucking doing. You don't get that money out, I'll use your fucking skull to open it the rest of the way." I nudged her on the back of the head with my fist. Judith dropped to her knees as I tossed her a sack that I found under the front counter. Judith pulled huge stacks of cash from the hole, slicing her arm on the jagged hot metal in the prosses. After a few seconds, the sack was so full that the two strings wouldn't reach one another to tie the bag.

"It's full, we should go!"

I snatched the bag from Judith's grip, then threw it over my shoulder. "No fucking shit, bitch." I said kicking her as she tried to get back to her feet.

"This is Sheriff Chuck Daniels. Put down your weapons and come out with your hands in the air!"

I smiled the biggest smile I had ever smiled in my entire life. "This is the moment I've been waiting for." I said happily as I drew the scorpion revolver and ducked under one of the broken windows.

"I'm afraid that's not going to happen, Sheriff. I advise you and your men to just fuck off, or whole lot of you are going to die here today." I knew they weren't going anywhere, and that's exactly what I had hoped for.

Chapter 7
Dead Or Alive

"Eight lawmen lost their lives that day. Eight good lawmen with families. You also managed to kill three civilians. Two of them were mothers of young children. How the hell do you live with yourself after something like that?"

It looked like the old sheriff was about to cry like a bitch. I wish he had. "You know, in the greater scheme of things, what does it matter? Thousands of babies are born every day. Those people have already been replaced a hundred times over."

The sheriff looked up at me like I had just insulted his mother. *"Every human life on this planet matters, maybe, except the lives of those who kill indiscriminately for no rhyme or reason. My question is, how in the hell did you escape? When the Marshalls found your armor on the bank floor, it was riddled with dents and dings. How did you get out of the bank unscathed?"*

I thought back on the battle. I remembered every face of every sorry motherfucker I dropped that day. "I guess those lawmen that you so highly praise weren't the decorated protectors of the peace that you paint them out to be." I grinned at the sheriff, knowing I was getting under his skin. He sighed, then surprised me with a smile.

"You didn't make it too far though, did you? Those Murphree brothers caught up with you. They kicked your ass something fierce. But you were found alone, no Judith in sight. Where was she then? And most importantly, where is she now?"

I stood up from the cot to stretch my legs and back out a bit, the sheriff watched me like a queer bull ready to fuck. "Damn, sheriff. Why do you feel such a need to jump ahead? Isn't my story and where were at in it captivating enough to keep you interested? Maybe its not me trapped in a cell right now, maybe it's you that's the prisoner, a prisoner of your own will to do good for the worthless scum around you."

The sheriff ran his liver spotted hand over his thick white mustache before stuffing another wad of chewing tobacco in his lower lip. This man reminded me of an old dog. An old dog that had lived a full life, and now lived in agony in his later years. Someone needed to take this old dog out and put him down.

"You know something, Harley? You may be right about me. But the only difference is, I can walk out of my prison

anytime I want. My prison isn't one step closer to a rope around my neck."

Bullets dinged off the armor as I raised up from the window. I fired the scorpion revolver, hitting three lawmen. I managed to hit two in the chest and one in the face. I took cover as pieces of brick exploded around from the shotgun blasts. I raised back up once the shooting ceased. I fired three more shots, hitting three more lawmen. I ducked back down for the next onslaught. I opened the cylinder, quickly sliding in six more bullets. The idiots stopped to reload their pussy shooters again. I cut two more of them down with ease.

"Pull back!" I heard one of the lawmen shout from outside. I raised up again, but was caught off guard by Judith firing the shotgun from the window on the other side of the room. A woman screamed after the first shot, then went silent after the second.

"Who the hell are you shooting at?" I asked curiously.

Judith turned around; a maniacal, bloodthirsty look emerged. *"There were two whores hiding on the side of the building. I assume you don't want any witnesses."*

I laughed harder than I ever had. "I'm the most wanted outlaw in the entire country. Everyone already knows who I am and what I look like, but good work."

I gave Judith a thumbs-up which seemed to make her legitimately happy for a moment. "I'm glad to see that you're having fun. Now we need to get the fuck out of here." I nodded towards the back door. We crawled on our hands and knees just in case someone wanted to play hero.

"I can't believe they gave up so easily." Judith mumbled as she tossed her empty shotgun to the side. I removed my armor, amazed how many bullets had actually struck me.

"They didn't give up, they just pulled back to call for reinforcements. They'll have this bank surrounded with a lynch-mob in about five-minutes."

Judith and I made our way out the back door and onto our horses. Once we were up the hill behind the bank and back into the plains, I turned to appreciatethe destruction I had caused. Lawmen and townsfolk ran towards the bank, rifles and shotguns in hand, ready to cut me down. The bodies of the fallen lay scattered on the street, now soulless packs of spoiled meat.

"Are we taking some of the money to Gunner's mother?" Judith asked from behind me while I enjoyed the show.

I turned to her, annoyed that she would ask something so unintelligent. "Gunner was a fucking simpleton. His mother is some whore still sucking cocks at the brothel in White Water. Bitch isn't seeing a single cent from me."

I could tell Judith was starting to come down from her rampaging high, her face looking empty and lifeless once more. *"Well, what are you going to do with all that money? Are you going to give up this life? Seems like enough money to get away and never be found."*

I heard the scream of a woman in town as she dropped to her knees, crying over what I assumed was her dead husband. "I'm not doing anything with this fucking money, bitch. I'll use some of it to buy some supplies from the general store in Rockford, then burn the rest of it when winter rolls around."

Judith looked surprised as she ran her hands through the sack of bills. *"Burn it? Why in the world would you do that? There is so much you could do with this, so much good you could do the world."*

I turned quickly, smacking Judith in the face as hard as I could. Her legs came out from under her, sending her to the ground below. "You fucking parasite!" I screamed as I kicked her in the ass as she tried to stand back up. "I take what I want. I'm not a slave like those worthless motherfuckers down there." I pointed at Damnation; my eyes burned like hot lava. "People like you are the ones who need this manmade bullshit to live. Look where money got you. Fucking nowhere except facedown under my boot.

"You said you were using some of it to buy supplies at a general store. That makes you no different than me or the people down there."

I scoffed at the stupid bitch. "The only reason I'm using this outhouse shit paper to buy from the general store in Redrock is because the owner helped me out of a predicament a few years ago. It would be in bad taste to steel from someone who's shown you a kindness." It was hard to keep a straight face when proclaiming my loyalty to another human being.

"You don't give a rat's ass about anyone but yourself. You're nothing but a hypocrite and snake in the grass!"

Judith tried to stand once more to make her point. I kicked her in the ass, sending her tumbling into a shallow sinkhole that I hadn't noticed before then. "Speaking the truth doesn't always work out in one's favor."

I chuckled as I kicked dirt and grass into her stupid face. "Well, I guess this is as good a time as any. Anything else you'd like to say before I put you out of your fucking misery?" I pulled out the scorpion revolver and aimed it at Judith's crotch area. It felt like aiming a weapon at a rabid animal.

"I see right through you."

I shrugged my shoulders at her final words before pulling back the hammer with my thumb. Judith closed her eyes, bracing herself for her uncertain death. Before I could pull the trigger, the sinkhole collapsed in, sending Judith screaming into the dark abyss.

"Holy fuck!" I backed up so that I wouldn't suffer the same fate. I looked down into the hole. I didn't hear Judith's screams any more.

I thought about her body being eaten by the worms below, the foul stench that would attract animals to her rotting corpse. "At least you'll finally be worth something." I said with a smile before holstering my pistol. I glanced over at Sticky's old horse; I might as well get rid of it too. "Come here, girl." I said softly as I led the horse towards the gaping sinkhole. The stubborn horse didn't want to jump on its own, so I decided to put a bullet in both of its front legs. I shoved the whining horse into the hole and watched it disappear into the darkness, just like Judith had.

The sun was starting to set, and I knew that I couldn't set up camp so close to town again. Surely the angry citizens of Damnation would be hunting me before too long. I loaded up my belongings and headed north towards Redrock. I only made it a few miles before stopping near the San Luis River to fill my canteen and give Davis a much-needed rest. I looked out over the river as the water trickled slowly downstream, the setting sun checking its reflection one last time before disappearing over the hills.

I thought about what life must be like for these mindless fucks who work hard everyday of their lives, paying taxes, buying meaningless shit to keep the bitch at home happy so she doesn't go out and suck on your neighbor's pecker. All of that work, all of that time and energy spent, only to lose it all in death.

Once the sun was gone, the bull frogs started yapping back and forth at one another. I read once that the American bullfrog lays eggs that look like a jelly like mass that floats on the surface of the water. They can lay up to twenty-thousand eggs at a time.

"Maybe we'll grab us some books in Redrock." I said to Davis as he slurped loudly on the river side.

"Get them hands in the air, pardner."

I froze at the sound of another man's voice behind me. The hammer on his pistol cocked back slowly. "Have you thought this through?" I asked, raising my hands and placing them behind my neck.

"Keep yer fuckin' mouth shut. Yer worth thirty-thousand dollars right now; twenty if yer dead. Don't think for a second that I give a shit which amount lines my pockets. Get on yer feet, keep yer arms raised."

I did as I was told for the time being. I couldn't wait to end this cocksucker's miserable life. "How did you find me all the way out here, all by yourself?" The miserable prick popped me on the back of the head with the grip of his pistol, knocking my hat into the mud.

"Who says I'm alone?"

The mystery hero pulled on my coat, turning my body to face him.

"Well, look at that. More cocksuckers." I laughed at the four men standing behind me with their guns pointed. "The infamous Murphree brothers."

I shook my head and rolled my eyes sarcastically. I wasn't going to show this group of uneducated retards any mercy when the time came. The one who had turned me around looked to be the oldest of the Murphree's. His name was Skip, or something like that. The Murphree's were a group of bounty hunting brothers who came down from the Appalachian Mountains. They were feared by every outlaw and gunslinger in the territory, and for a damn good reason. The Murphree's were the reason so many outlaws and bandits had faced judgment for their sins. Though I would never admit it, I knew I was fucked.

"We got us a good one. We've had our eyes out for ole Harley Heck for a long time. Who'da thought we'd find him

on the side of a river, staring off at the sunset like a primo faggot?"

The Murphree's were a ruthless group of individuals, but they were undoubtably as dumb as a bag of severed cocks. "Four cowboys sleeping together in the same tent every night under the stars isn't considered 'queer' where you fellas come from?" I asked with a sly smirk. I was instantly slapped across the face with Skip's navy revolver.

"If you know what's good for ya, you'll keep your trap shut until you're safe in a jail cell."

Skip was the oldest, but also the smallest of the four. The other three had a young, scrappy look about them. They weren't nearly as levelheaded as the eldest brother, who continued locking eyes with me until he went to his horse to fetch a pair of shackles. I drew my scorpion revolver, clipping one of the brothers on the far left in the neck. I aimed at the next one but was quickly disarmed before I could get a shot off. The beating I took after apparently killing the youngest of the four Murphree's, was legendary. I took kick after kick to the face and body, my head was shoved under water and held until I started to pass out.

"It's a damn shame to put down such a beauty."

My head was forced to the side so that I could watch Skip put a bullet in Davis's face. Davis neighed loudly before taking another bullet in the side of the head. My only friend in the world dropped to his front knees, then face first into the river. I watched the blood flow down stream as his huge body twitched a few times before resting permanently still.

"You didn't have to do that." I growled before my head was shoved back into the water. I took a further beating with a whip that the middle brother kept on his horse, the pain was so unbearable that I passed out a few times during the fifteen or so lashes I received. The youngest brother was buried up on a hill in the plains, I belched as loud as I could after the three brothers said their amens.

"That's too fancy of a weapon for a piece of shit like you."

I was slapped across the face a few times with my scorpion revolver before Skip tucked it away in his saddle bag. I was lassoed and tossed on the back of a scrawny nag owned by one of the brothers. I think the brother's name was Cricket.

"You're lucky we like to turn boys like you in alive. I oughta twist yer damn head off yer body and fuck yer neck real good." The third brother said as he spat in my face.

"What's your name?" I asked the brother as he wiped his chin of excess spit. The brother I was yet to learn the name of grabbed me tightly by the back of the hair.

"Names Gecko, don't forget it."

Under the cool guy façade, I made sure to smile. "Oh, I won't."

Chapter 8

Scum Boys

"And that is how I ended up in this little slice of heaven." I smiled at the sheriff who had tossed his notepad on his desk and unbuttoned the top button of his white dress shirt. "Your buddies, the Murphree's, beat my ass the whole two-day trip. They didn't allow me to eat, sleep, or even have a single thought to myself. The fact that they allowed me to live was a testament to their impractical moral code."

The tired old sheriff looked as if he had had enough for the day. *"Well, at least we know about where Judith's body is. Her family can finally sleep at night. It's a damn shame that poor girl was so corrupted by your sick mind, a real shame. As for the shit you endured on the way here, I applaud those three boys. Hell, I might even send them the noose we use to hang you with tomorrow, just as an added thank you."*

The sheriff dimmed the lantern he had been using for light before grabbing his big gay cowboy hat from a tiny hook by the front door.

"Enjoy your final night alive."

The sheriff turned and walked out the door, locking it behind him. The tiny sheriff's office was now so quiet you could hear a church mouse orgasm. I whistled a song I heard my pa singing one time back when I was a boy. A flood of memories came crashing down on my head as I closed my eyes.

"I'll tell you about the crazed group of Injuns that we fought off during the war. They were the nastiest group of crazed motherfuckers this side of the border."

I listened in awe at my father's war stories, they were always so colorful and fascinating. I crossed my legs while I sat on the floor of the cabin, my heart racing with anticipation.

"I and a small patrol group I led were held-up in an old fort they kept prisoners in during the start of the war. The place was mostly burnt down, but still made for good cover at night. You never wanted to be out in them woods sleepin'. Good way to get your throat sliced open by some renegade Indians who hadn't quite learned their place in society. We were informed, before we left, to keep a lookout for a group

of Injuns known amongst the confederacy as the scum boys. They were a nasty gang of ruffians who took no prisoners and showed no mercy to those who were unlucky enough to cross their path. They were said to wear all white face paint that would glow under the moonlight. People said they looked like the ghosts of the fallen Comanche when they would appear from the darkness."

The hairs on the back of my neck stood up as my father continued his story.

"The boys and I held up in that old fort for the night, slept down in a secret bunker below it. It was a place they kept extra ammunition and supplies. No one outside of the confederacy knew about it."

My pa spit a long sticky stream of spit from his mouth and onto the cabin floor, my ma side-eyed him as she shook her head, disapproving of his filthy habits.

"I woke up in the middle of the night. I had to piss something fierce. I climbed up the ladder that led to the old captain's office above ground. It was colder than a dead whore's pussy out there that night. I wanted to hurry up and do my business before my nuts shriveled up inside my body. I was gone maybe three or four minutes. When I returned to the captain's office, the hatch that I had closed was now opened. The screams of my men stopped me from putting even my big toe on the first step of that ladder. I didn't have my Colt *navy on my hip, left it down below like some dipshit private would. I hid myself behind some wooden crates, hoping and praying that whoever was down there wouldn't find me. After all the screaming stopped, I heard the wooden ladder creaking. The tiny room filled up with light from their torches, their shadows like giant demons coming to drag us to hell. They were speaking to each other in their Injun mumbo jumbo, I knew they were looking for me."*

I pictured my pa cowering in the room while the Indians searched for him. I could see it on his face that it terrified him to even recount such a memory. "Did they find you, Pa?" I asked curiously. Pa looked down at me from his rocking chair, I could tell right away that he was annoyed.

"If they found me, I'd be dead. If I were dead, you wouldn't exist. What kind of stupid question is that?"

Pa stomped his foot on the cabin floor as hard as he could. A chill went down my spine. Pa's fuse was a short one, I knew better than to provoke him.

"Just shut your goddamn mouth and let me finish. You're an ungrateful little shit, you know that?"

I lowered my head in shame.

"I watched those Injuns carry my platoon's bodies up one by one. Once they had them in a big pile outside in the middle of the fort, they set them on fire, then danced around the burning corpses. I'll never forget those painted white faces

with smears of black under their eyes. I had to watch them celebrate their victory as the smell of burning flesh reminded me how hungry I was. I could have snuck back underground and grabbed my pistol. I could have taken those sons of bitches to hell, but I didn't move until the sun came up."

My Pa looked back at my mother as he rubbed his crotch area. I had no idea why he was doing something so strange. I rubbed my crotch as well. I ended up getting slapped across the face and was forced to sleep outside. I watched through the window that night as Ma got down on her knees and put Pa's penis in her mouth. She sucked on it until Pa let out a loud moan, grabbing Ma's hair and pulling her face further towards his region.

"You suck such a good dick. You're a fucking pro."

My father glanced up and caught me spying, he just winked as he shoved Ma to the floor. His penis dripped thick white gunk from the tip of it. I wondered what in the hell that stuff was.

"Rise and shine, sleepyhead."

My eyes shot open at the sound of my cell door being unlocked and opened. The sheriff stood next to my bed with two armed deputies. An exhilarated smile shown under his white mustache.

"No breakfast?" I asked, sitting up and putting my hat on. I could almost feel the sheriff's excitement radiating off him.

"It's time for you to go and see the judge. Don't worry, it'll be short and sweet. We don't want to keep a celebrity like yourself waiting."

I was yanked up from my cot and thrown against the cell wall by the two deputies. "Easy, I don't want you messing up my pubes before the judge has a chance to put my cock in his mouth." A sharp punch to the back made my knee buckle.

"Watch your mouth, prisoner." One of the deputies shouted as he put his knee to the back of my neck, pancaking me against the brick wall.

"My bad, I didn't know you fellas were so fucking sensitive." My head was smacked against the wall so hard that I spat two of my teeth out on the floor. I was lifted to my feet and dragged out the front door. The sheriff stayed close behind with a bolt action rifle pointed at my back.

As I was forced down the street, the townsfolk peered through shop windows. Those outside stopped to whisper to one another.

"I'm guessing your judge has already made up his mind. Why the hell are you wasting time taking me to see him?" I asked, not trying to be a smart-ass for once. Even still, my shackled hands were pulled so far up my back that my fingers touched the spot between my shoulders.

"Keep your goddamn mouth shut!"

I imagined all the wonderful things I would do to these cocksuckers. One of my fantasies involved decapitating them using those badges they hid behind.

"Looks like a good turn-out."

The sheriff pointed up at the hill just outside of town. I looked to where he was pointing to see three horses standing side by side, the remaining Murphree brothers staring down at me. "Careful fellas. They might be here to kill me themselves, might think the noose isn't enough for the likes of ole Harley Heck." I laughed as the deputies pushed my hands up even further.

"You open that mouth of yours one more time, you won't make it to the gallows."

I was walked into an alley in between the feedstore and the annex building, then shoved through a side door and into a small room containing a few bookshelves and a desk. My eye caught a book I had read a few years back. It was the introduction to the theory of law. An insightful, yet droll read. Another door opened, and in walked a short old man with frizzy grey hair and a slight hunch. I smirked at the confederate flag eyepatch that covered his right eye. How and why would a judge wear such garbage? Especially one who seems to be an avid reader of such educational literature. The judge sat down at his desk without looking up at me.

"Your Pa was a great man. Shame he isn't here to see the low life his only son has become."

The Judge's voice was raspy and harsh on the ears.

"You sully his name with the atrocities you've committed, you should be ashamed of yourself."

The judge finally looked up at me, his only visible eye was as gray as his unbrushed hair.

"I guess if I had committed these 'atrocities' during a war, I would be given a gold metal and a handshake. I'm sure I haven't done a single thing that you and my dick head father hadn't done a million times over."

The room grew quiet. That was, until I was cracked in the back of the head by the butt of a bolt action rifle.

"Shut it!" The sheriff growled from behind me.

"We did what was best for our country during the war. You better watch how you speak, boy. Your father and I fought for what was right, we fought for the values this country was built on."

My head throbbed and I knew I was going to be hit again, but I couldn't resist. "You and those like you have no idea what 'values' are. You're an entitled racist. Nothing more, nothing less." The judge held up his hand, I assumed to stop the sheriff from cracking the back of my skull open.

"I guess we have us a nigger loving outlaw in our presence." The judge mumbled as he pulled out a stack of papers from his desk drawer. I clenched my fists as I imagined stomping this fucker's skull to pieces.

"I find it amusing that someone so morally corrupted is allowed to Judge the morality of others." I said as I leaned forward in the chair I was forced to sit in. The judge looked up at me, his one eye burning with hatred. I was a bug that needed to be squished.

"Let's see; you raped innocent women, you killed children, you murdered for your personal amusement, you stole, and you fucking loved it. How are you and I any different, apart from you being a racist fucking prick?"

I was cracked in the head once more by the sheriff.

"I've made up my mind. Hang this traitor."

The judge gestured to the deputies to take me away. "Back at it again, huh?" I said as I spat on the floor in front of the judge's desk. "Guess I'll be seeing you in hell." I winked as I was pushed through the door leading back into the alley. As soon as my boots hit the dirt I was kicked in the back of the leg, then punched so hard that I could hear my jaw crunch like gravel under a wagon tire.

"I'd give anything to put you down right here and now!"

One of the deputies pulled the hammer back on his Colt, shoving the tip of the barrel into my right temple.

"Fucking do it! I'll come back with a fucking vengeance. I'll rape everything you stand for!" I hissed, spitting blood in the dirt.

"Lower your weapon!" The sheriff shouted, pushing the deputy's gun out of my face.

"We have a responsibility as public servants to see that this man pays in accordance with the law. We will not preform an execution in the middle of the goddamn street!"

I looked up at the sheriff, who was now red in the face and screaming at his inexperienced deputies. "You know something, you and I are more alike than I thought."

The sheriff looked down at me in disgust. *"You and I are nothing alike. You're a rabid dog who needs to be put down."*

I shrugged my shoulders as I was pulled back to my feet. "That's where you're wrong. You and I are alike in the sense that we both stay true to what we are."

The sheriff ignored me as he ordered his men to take me to the gallows. A small crowd had started to form. There's nothing like a public execution to bring folks together.

Chapter 9
Fitted Necktie

"You know, if you hadn't killed everyone in your life, you might have someone to miss you when you're buried. The only reason I'll be at your funeral is to make sure you stay dead."

The sheriff didn't look too sad to see the fitted necktie fastened around my throat.

"Better keep that six-shooter aimed at me when the preacher is rambling. I might jump up and bite you."

I smiled as the executioner walked up the steps of the gallows. He was a huge, beefy man, his chest covered in thick black hair. "Looks like my carriage awaits." I whispered to the sheriff, who still stood before me. The executioner made it to the top step, a black hood covered his face. The only thing I could see were a pair of hollow black eyes.

"It's been a pleasure." The sheriff tipped his hat at me before stepping to the side to better address the audience. I felt an emptiness in my gut as I stared at the townspeople

before me, the hatred was so thick in the air that I could physically taste it.

"Ladies and gentlemen. We are gathered here today to witness the execution of Harley James Heck. Heck is charged and has been found guilty of the following crimes. One-hundred-and-twenty counts of Murder, armed robbery of eleven stagecoaches and three banks, raping indiscriminately, assault on a peace officer, kidnapping, horse theft, trespassing, animal cruelty, disturbing the peace, arson, perjury, and assault."

I had almost dozed off if not for the stench of the executioner's horrid body odor.

"Do you have any last words before your sentence is carried out?"

The sheriff turned to me as the whispers in the crowd came to a dead stop. I looked around for a moment I was quite impressed with the turnout. "I would like to say one thing before my neck is broken and I hang here like a Christmas ornament in the middle of this cunt fucking town."

The crowd gasped all at once.

"I would like to say that it was all worth it, and I wouldn't change a fucking thing."

The crowd gasped once again.

"Hang the bastard!"

"Kill him!"

"Rot in hell!"

"Pull the lever!"

I couldn't help but smile at the positive reaction of my diehard fans. The Executioner grabbed the wooden handle that would open the hatch beneath me. but stopped like he had forgotten something. A sack was pulled over my head, the opening tucked into the thick rope around my neck. I saw the executioner's sweaty hand grip the wooden handle; the crowd grew silent right before the floor beneath me disappeared. My body dropped for what felt like an eternity before coming to a neck snapping halt. The crowd cheered as I fought for breath. They celebrated as my legs flailed wildly. They moaned in disappointment as my body went still.

My mind started fading as I prepared to meet old man death. A loud shot rang out before I felt my body hit the ground below. The sounds of people screaming came flooding in as quickly as the oxygen I had been deprived of over the last few seconds. Another shot rang out, a thud on the gallows above me sounded like the executioner had taken a bullet to the head.

"Clear out! Everyone get back to your homes!" The sheriff called as his pistol fired back towards the invisible assassin.

More shots rang out, the sound of bodies falling from the gallows and hitting the dirt below was unmistakable. Who in the hell had saved me from hanging? And why in the hell didn't they do it sooner? After a few minutes, the shooting along with the shouting, stopped.

"You don't know what you're doing. Please, you don't have to do this!"

The sound of the sheriff pleading with the perpetrator was music to my ears. A single shot and the sheriff went quiet.

"Hello?" I called out to the sound of footsteps approaching me. Through the sack I could see the silhouette of a figure standing before me. "Untie these motherfucking ropes and get this bag off my goddamn head!"

The figure just stood there, not uttering a single word. More footsteps approached us, meaning that my guardian angel wasn't alone. "I told you to take this fucking sack off my head!" I shouted as I became increasingly more frustrated. I felt two sets of arms wrap around my body, lifting me up and carrying me away. "What in the fuck are you doing? Untie me!" I growled as I fought against the shadowy figures. "I'll make each of you suck the white crust from the crevasses of my dick if you don't take this fucking sack off my goddamn head!"

My body was thrown into the back of a wagon.

"Yumuhkitu."

My ass hole clenched when I heard the distinct voice of a male Comanche warrior.

"Fuck." I muttered to myself as the wagon started moving forward. We traveled for what felt like most of the day. I could tell the sun had set from the cool breeze and the sound of crickets singing over the creaking wagon and the neighing horses. My hands had gone numb a few hours ago. I couldn't even feel the tips of my fingers by this point. For just a moment I could hear the voices of two Comanche, they laughed as if one had made a funny joke.

"Where are you taking me?" I called out as loud as I could. The wagon came to a sudden stop. "Hello?" I asked as I felt hands grabbing my legs and ankles, dragging me from the bed of the wagon.

I hit the ground with a thud. It hurt like hell, considering my hands were still tied behind my back. I was placed down on my ass once I was carried to wherever we were going. There was a silence in the air for a few moments before I could see torches being lit around me. "I'm going to fucking skin you alive!" I went to shout before the sack was ripped from my head. It took my eyes a moment to adjust, but when they finally did, I couldn't believe what stood before me.

Chapter 10
A Goddamned Legend

I REMEMBERED A WOMAN I met a few years back, right after I sealed my gang in a cave to die excruciating deaths. I had set-up camp on the edge of Black Bone Forest. I did so because I knew I wouldn't have to deal with any unwanted visitors in the night.

Black Bone Forest was an old dead forest a few miles outside of Cranberry, a small logging town with a small population. The residents of Cranberry feared the forest due to an urban legend that had started over a hundred years ago, something about an old witch that lived in a cave somewhere out there.

I had been on the run for over a week. I desperately needed a place to lay low until the heat died down. The forest was always dark, even during the sunniest days when the sun was highest in the sky, the woods stayed dark. The trees were all paper birch, which obviously added a creepy factor to its eerie history. I looked up at the night sky as I rested next to the roaring fire I had built. Davis kept tugging at his reins that I had secured to a thick stump. I had never seen him act that way, he seemed uneasy and frightened.

"Mind if I join ya?"

I drew my pistol so fast that my holster came with it. A woman wearing in a strange attire walked out of the darkness like the forest had just given birth to her.

"Who the fuck are you? What are you doing wandering around these parts this late at night?" I wasn't an easy man to scare, but goddamn, this bitch scared the fuck out of me when she popped up like the way she did. She stared at my fire for a few moments before taking an uninvited seat on a dead log across from me.

"Are you listening to me, woman?" I asked, still aiming my six-shooter in her direction.

The bitch continued staring at the flames. Her face reminded me of a doll I saw in a shop window when I was a boy.

"It's so nice meeting new people. I don't see many faces around here. The wolves are the only thing wandering around these woods this late."

The woman still hadn't looked me in the eyes. She just stared at the damn fire.

"I came here to be left alone. I didn't think anyone lived around here."

I lowered my piece; the creepy bitch didn't seem to be a threat for the time being. The longer I looked at her, the more I realized how pretty she was. It could have been the fact that I hadn't been inside a bitch in the past few days.

"Do you feel alone?" she asked, finally looking up at me.

"I don't know. I prefer it. When you're alone, there's no one around to disappoint you." I shifted upwards because my ass cheeks had fallen asleep. "You really shouldn't just walk up on strange men sitting by themselves. Especially men that look like me." I laughed to myself.

"What's your name?" I asked scooting closer to her.

"Vera." She whispered with a sly smile.

"That's a pretty name for an even prettier girl." I stood up from the ground. Vera just sat there staring up at me like she was waiting for something. "Are you retarded or something?" I asked, standing just inches from where she sat. I looked around the darkness for a moment to make sure she didn't have a man with her. "There's no way that a sane woman who is as beautiful as you are- is just walking alone out here."

I looked at the woman's stupid outfit. A white bonnet rested on her hark brown hair. "Are you one of those Amish girls from Cranberry?" I asked, studying her outfit. Vera didn't respond, she just continued staring up at me. "I guess if you don't want to talk, we can do other stuff you probably don't want to be doing." I kicked Vera in the face as hard as I could.

"Ugh!" She cried out as she held onto the orbital bone that I undoubtably smashed to pieces. I kicked her in the face again, the hand that covered her eye crunched under my dirty boot. I lifted up her ugly navy-blue dress. She was naked underneath.

"Look at that bush!" I admired Vera's pussy beard. I reached down and stroked my fingers through it. "I may have been wrong about you. It's pretty obvious that this is what you wanted. Why else would you come over here? You're hunting for some good dick, someone to break you." I grabbed a handful of her pussy hair; I ripped it out with one swift tug. Vera screamed so loudly that Davis started kicking his back legs up in the air. I held the handful of blood and pubes up to my nose, it smelled like fresh flowers.

"Daddy!" Vera cried out as blood and snot ran down her pretty little mouth.

"That's right. I'm your daddy." I pulled off my gun belt, folding it the way my father used to fold the leather strap he would hit me with when I stepped out of line. I smacked Vera's pasty white ass until it was covered in thick whelps. Her screams grew louder and louder. I pulled down my pants, my cock was as hard as it had ever been. I knew

I wouldn't be able to cum, I never fucking could. But I would enjoy this, regardless. I pulled my hunting knife from my boot, the flames from the fire danced in the silver blade. I grabbed Vera by the hair, ripping off her stupid white bonnet. I cut into her neck until the screaming stopped. After a few minutes of sawing, her headless body dropped to the ground. I held her head up so that I could see her pretty face.

"It looks like you're still screaming." I laughed as I shoved my dirty cock into her gapping mouth. I fucked Vera's head for an hour straight. I wanted to fucking cum.

"Goddamn it!" I shouted as I tossed Vera's severed head into the darkness. I used her nude corpse as a bed that night, I hadn't slept so good in years. The next morning rode into Cranberry to have a shot of whisky before heading back out.

"Did you hear? Crawford's daughter didn't come home last night."

I glanced over at the man in dirty overalls talking to the bartender.

"The retarded one?" the bartender replied, *"She's always wanderin' off. I'm sure she'll find her way back home before too long."*

"Crawford and his other daughter, I think her name is Judy or Judith, they're out lookin for her."

I smiled to myself before tossing a silver dollar on the bar before leaving Cranberry for good.

I stared at the ghost that stood before me, the flames from the torches illuminating her hate filled expression. "You had a sister named Vera, didn't you?" I asked Judith as she stood side by side with the Scum Boys from my father's story. Judith looked like Hell had swallowed her and spit her back out.

"How did you find out?" I asked curiously.

Judith's expression never altered as she stepped slowly towards me. She kneeled down, putting her hand on my shoulder. *"I've known all along, you piece of shit. I saw you leaving that day at the saloon. I saw that smile on your murdering face. It wasn't hard to guess it was the wanted outlaw wandering through Cranberry like his shit didn't stink. I've spent the last few years tracking you down. I finally found you and your boy's hiding out in that canyon."*

I scoffed at the idiotic shit that spewed from this whore's cock socket. "Bitch, we found you. You didn't find dick."

Judith patted my shoulder with a devious smile. *"That's what you think. Did you not find it strange that I never tried to run? Did it seem odd to you that I stuck around? For a smart man, you sure are oblivious."*

I looked around at the Comanche, their faces covered with the white paint that my Pa mentioned in his story. They looked even fucking creepier in person. "Why are they with you? Are they friends of yours? Are they passing that white pussy around?"

Judith looked at the Comanche Scum Boys that stood ominously behind her. *"I was on the verge of death when they found me in that sink hole you pushed me in. The Comanche seem to have a sixth sense when they find someone seeking revenge like I was. A group of confederate soldiers attacked their land during the war, they raped and killed their women and children with no remorse. They took their pound of flesh one night in an abandoned fort. I guess since then, they are more than accommodating when someone needs to kill a white man."*

I couldn't believe the shit I was hearing. My father never attacked these assholes, they attacked his platoon without provocation. "And how did these savages feed you this horseshit? Are you fluent in their yip yap?"

Judith smiled. *"We're approaching the year nineteen hundred. They've been around enough white people to catch on to our language."*

A few of the Comanche laughed along with Judith. This only angered me further. "Okay, bitch. You got me. Now what?"

Judith looked back at the Scum Boys. I could tell that my fate had already been decided upon.

"Does this spot look familiar?"

I looked around for a second, squinting to see past the dark patches. "Were back in the plains, same place I threw you away like the used-up trash that you are."

I glanced at the huge hole that sat just a few feet from me. "So, are you just going to toss me down the hole and spend everyday of the rest of your pathetic life praying to god that I don't climb up and rip your fucking tits off!?"

I found myself growing more and more angry. The thought of this cunt besting me didn't sit well.

"No, Harley. My new friends here are going to torture you until you beg them to end your sorry ass life. Then I'm going to toss what's left of you down the hole."

Judith smiled at me as three of the Comanche approached with tomahawks. I winked at Judith as the first swing caught me in the face, splitting the bridge of my nose open. The middle Comanche struck me in the jaw, leaving another gruesome gash. The third shot caught my bad eye just enough to split the cornea and reach the pupil. I sat there and took it, not giving Judith the satisfaction of my suffering. I felt blood running down my face and neck. I was already blind in my bad eye beforehand, so fuck it.

"Why won't you scream for me?" Judith asked, kneeling down and shoving her fingernail into my mangled eyeball. I had never felt physical pain like this in my entire life. I wanted to fucking scream but didn't.

"Eat shit, you stupid cunt." I spat in her face. I yearned to mutilate her bloody corpse. "I'm going to eviscerate you. You know that, right?" I asked before one of the Skip used his hatchet to sever my right hand. My jaw clenched and my one good eye watered, the pain was ungodly.

"Would you boys be so kind as to pull his pants down?" Judith asked one of the Scum Boys with a cunty little grin.

"Years of being the most feared tribe in the country, and now you take orders from a fucking woman." I said, trying to block out the pain.

The Comanche Scum Boys looked at each other and then back at me. "How far you've fallen." I said, laughing.

My pants were ripped down and my ass was made to stick straight up in the air like a cheap whore. "You going to fuck me as good as I fucked you?" I asked Judith as I inadvertently inhaled dirt.

"Yeah, I'm going to fuck you really good, Harley."

Judith learned down to show me what she planned to ram up my ass.

"You're going to pay for this, you hear me, bitch?"

Judith walked slowly to my rear as two of the Comanche held my head down in the dirt and dead grass.

"This is for my sister."

With all her might, Judith shoved the head of a live rattlesnake as far up my shit hole as she could. I felt its fangs clamp down. Its tail rattled vociferously, but my scream was even worse.

Chapter 11
Den Of Serpents

Having a rattlesnake bite the inside of my asshole made me wish I had just died on the gallows. The world around me was green. I rubbed my face in the grass to try and clear my vison.

"Where are you, white man?"

I was surrounded by ghosts. I tried to stand, but my legs had become useless stumps, existing only to be gawked at.

"You're good for nothing! You're no son of mine!"

My father grabbed me by the throat. I could no longer breathe. "Please, please, Pa. Let me go!"

The ghosts continued laughing at me, a tall demon with yellow eyes stood with them, she held a giant serpent.

"Get the hell away from me!" I reached my hand up to block the creatures, but my hand had been replaced with my mother's head.

"Climb in bed with your Ma. I'll kiss you goodnight."

My mother's mouth opened as thick hairy spiders crawled out of it and onto her face. "Ma!" I cried out as

I tried to push her head from my hand. The ghosts and the giant creature started moving closer and closer. I felt broken glass crunching under my weight. "I'm bleeding!" I cried out with the voice of a small child. A hand came out from the ground beside me, grabbing me by the shirt.

"Do you feel alone?"

The rotted face of Vera came from the dirt. Her lips had been chewed off and maggots dripped from her empty eye sockets.

"I can make you cum better than my sister."

Vera opened her mouth, reaching for my exposed cock.

"Get the hell away from me!"

I shoved the rotted corpse that crumbled to pieces.

"Harley, you're melting."

Gunner was down next to me, his body crudely sewn back together with strands of barbed wire.

"I'm melting?" I asked him as I began to sweat profusely. "Why am I melting?" I asked Gunner, who took a huge bite from his burnt hand. He chewed and swallowed before turning to me.

"It must just be yer time to melt, Harley. My time has come and gone."

He laughed before turning to a pile of ash. I continued sweating. It felt as if I were sitting inside of a wood stove that had been left burning all night.

"Help!" I cried out as colorful ooze poured from my mouth and ears. The ooze was blue, green, purple, and yellow. I tried to wipe the rainbow sludge away but more and more continued to protrude from every orifice of my body.

"Harley!"

I looked up at the tall creature that held the serpent. She smiled to show me her jagged teeth.

"Fuck you!"

I reached for the pistol that wasn't there. My head continued to spin like I was rolling down a hill in an old whisky barrel. I crawled towards the hole in the field. I had to get away from this creature and her minions from hell. Suddenly, everything became clear.

"What- what the hell was that? What did you do to me?" I looked up at Judith and the Scum Boys. They stared at me with curious, yet amused eyes.

"The tomahawks were soaked in something that the Comanche call 'black honey'. I guess that, and the snake bite together sent you on one wild ride for a few minutes."

I lifted my arm; a bloody stump replaced my shooting hand. "Just fucking kill me." I mumbled as I realized that my miserable life was coming to an end.

"We're not finished with you yet."

I watched Judith release the rattlesnake into the brush. "You know, none of this bullshit matters. No one is going to remember you, bitch. I'm Harley Heck, the most notorious outlaw to ever live! People will remember my name!" I dragged myself to my feet. "No one gives a damn about any of you fucking losers. I'm a goddamn legend! You can't kill me, no one can fucking kill me!" I stretched my arms out like I could summon lightning.

To my dismay, Judith only smiled.

"We'll see about that."

The Comanche raised several bolt action rifles, aiming them like a lawless firing squad.

"Do it!" I shouted at the top of my lungs. A shot rang out, but it wasn't from a weapon being held by the present company. It came from somewhere else.

"Drop the rifles! We're here to collect the wanted outlaw that you see fit to execute unlawfully." The voice of the eldest Murphree brother called out over a large hill from behind us. I turned to see the three remaining brothers mounted on their horses, the same way they were before coming to witness me hang in Damnation.

"We can't do that. This son of a bitch doesn't deserve to die quickly. You boy's turn around and take yourselves elsewhere." Judith called out as the Comanche turned their rifles towards the Murphree brothers.

From out of nowhere, the Comanche opened fire. I ducked and rolled as quickly as I could. The Murphree's returned fire almost instantly, killing one of the Scum Boys when a bullet zipped through his forehead. The bullet that killed the Indian was from my scorpion revolver that Skip had taken from me down by the river. I needed it back.

As the shooting continued, I crawled to the side of the hill where the brothers took cover. I made sure to stay low so that they wouldn't catch a glimpse of my shadow in the dark.

"How in the hell am I supposed to kill the three of them with no weapon and one fucking hand?" I thought out loud. Then it hit me, my goddamn hunting knife was still tucked away in my boot. I had forgotten all about it, considering I had made a slit on the inside of my ropers to hide the damn thing. "This would've come in handy when I was locked in that damn cell." I said, frustratingly pulling the blade from its hiding spot. How could I have been such a fool? If I had escaped using this knife last night, I wouldn't be stuck in-between these cocksuckers trying to kill me.

"Pull back!" Judith called out after two more Comanche Scum Boys dropped dead.

I noticed Judith holding her ribs. She had been shot. I smiled as I watched her, and the last two remaining Comanche scurry off like dogs who had just been poked with a sharp stick.

"Look at em run!" The middle Murphree cheered as he fired his six-shooter into the night sky. I was a bit disappointed that Judith had given up so easily. I guess she planned to live tonight and fight tomorrow.

"Where's Heck?" Skip asked looking down below the steep hillside.

"Right here, motherfucker." I whispered. Skip and-fuck, I forgot the names of the other two. "Toss over the scorpion revolver and I won't slit your brothers fucking throat." I held my hunting knife tightly to the younger looking brethren's neck. I salivated at the thought of his blood spitting out all over his two pathetic kin.

"You kill him, you got no leverage. You'll be dead before you even realized what happened."

Skip continued aiming my own gun at me, threatening my life with the weapon I had killed so many with.

"Yeah, but then you'll be burying another brother next to the measly little fuck you already buried this week. Do you want to take that chance, Skip?"

I knew these stupid fucks were thick headed to give up so easily. All that pride will get them dead before sunup.

"Fuck it!"

I pulled the blade across the brother's throat. Blood sprayed several feet before Skip could let out a sorrowful cry of despair. Oh, his name was Cricket. I laughed at the fact that I remembered his name once he was a twitching corpse lying in the dirt. Before The other two brothers could collect themselves, I pulled the Cattleman revolver from Crickets gun belt. I put a bullet in Gecko's head, sending skull and brain matter spraying all over the dead grass. I shot My scorpion revolver from Skip's hand. He looked up at me in horror as his wasted exitance flashed before his eyes.

"Go on then. Get it over with."

Skip closed his as he dropped down to his knees. I walked towards him, picking up my beloved weapon of choice.

"I sure missed you, baby." I planted a wet kiss on the silver cylinder. "I'm not going to kill you, not yet at least." I tied my belt around my wrist, trying to stop the bleeding before I dropped dead.

"You got what you wanted. You're free. Just kill me, end this shit now!"

"I'm going to have to cauterize this fucker. You know, if you dick heads had shown up ten minutes earlier, I wouldn't have had a snake head shoved up my ass, and I would still have a hand."

I took the pistol and held it where my dick would be. I shoved the barrel into Skip's mouth. I thrusted back and forth as he gagged like an inexperienced teen cunt.

"You like that dick? I bet you can make me pop."

I wasn't accustomed to holding my six-shooter in my right hand, I accidentally pulled the trigger early. "Well, shit." I laughed as Skips' brains watered the dry grass behind him. His fat body fell with a thump as smoke rolled from his dead lips. I picked up Cricket's gun belt and put it around my waist. "Guess I need to head back to Damnation. Can't just leave my hat there."

I hopped on one of the horses. It wasn't Davis, but it would do for now. "Let's ride!" I called out as the horse jumped from the hill, running at a full sprint. The first thing I needed to do after fixing up this hand is get a new gang together. I have many plans for the townsfolk of Damnation. "I'm Harley fucking-"

The horse came out from under me after stepping into that goddamned sink hole. Its neck bent at an awkward angle before dropping into the darkness.

"FUCK!" I called out as I tried to grab onto something, but it was too late. I hit the bottom with a thud, my legs snapped loudly, the jagged bones pierced through my pants. I laid there, looking up at the small amount of moon light that shined down through the hole.

"GOD FUCKING DAMN IT!"

The stupid fucking horse lay next to me, its eyes slowly glazing over. I was a goddamn legend; I was the most notorious outlaw this country had ever seen. Now, I would die in some fucking hole in the middle of nowhere.

"Maybe this is what happened to Billy the kid." I pondered to myself.

I tried to roll over, maybe there was a way out of here. I felt a clump of dirt hit the ground next to me. Then another, and another. I looked up at the disappearing moonlight as the sinkhole caved in on top of me. Burying the legend of Harley Heck.

"Mister, are you alright?"

I opened my eyes to a filthy old man with a thick white beard kneeling over top of me. "What- what in the fuck?" I asked trying to sit up.

"I was over yonder in that mineshaft when I hert you hollerin' somethin' awful. Lucky for you I've been down her minin' for a few days."

I shook the dirt from my face. My entire body was broken and sore. "Can you just get me the fuck out of here?" I asked, feeling for my pistol, only to make sure it hadn't been buried under a mound of dirt.

"Yes um. I can throw ya in that there cart I got all mines tinkerin' tools in. Take ya to Cranberry. Doctor there will fix ya right up."

The old man's voice was giving me a headache. I would kill him once he got me out of this dirt filled hell.

"Are you from Cranberry?" I asked curiously as the old prospector began dragging me to safety.

"Damn skippy. Been there since before the war. No plans of leavin' no time soon."

I thought to myself over the sounds of my broken bones crunching beneath my dirt-covered flesh. "Do you know a man who had a retard for a daughter? Lost her some years back?" The prospector thought for a moment has he panted like a sun cooked hog, I hoped he didn't die of old age before I got the hell out of here.

"Oh, yes um. I know ole Mr. Crawford. He got elected mayor 'bout a year come May. Good man Mr. Crawford is. He went and set up that reservation for them Injuns, right outside Cranberry he did. He and that other girl of his do-good things for them poor people. Why you wantin' to know 'bout Mr. Crawford? He a friend of yers?"

I looked up at the prospector who had dragged me all the way out through a tight opening in the mineshaft wall and out into a larger open area. "I don't know him yet, but I've been pretty close to both of his daughters."

The prospector glanced at me quickly from the corner of his eye. "I cut one's head off and used her corpse as a bed."

The prospector's face twisted in horror as he came to the realization that he maybe shouldn't have rescued the stranger in the sinkhole.

"I'm thinking about doing something worse to the other little bitch of his when I find her."

TO BE CONTINUED...

Acknowledgements

Like always, thanks to my good friend and fellow author, Jason Nickey.

Thanks to Ashley Fox for being a fucking winner and helping out upcoming authors the way that she is doing.

Thank you to Chuck Nasty for... I guess for being so damn nasty.

A huge shoutout to all of my social media followers for believing in me.

About the Author

Stuart Bray was born in Louisville, Kentucky on September 11th, 1991. He now resides in Salem, Kentucky with his wife and two sons. Stuart published his first book 'The Heretic' in 2021. You can follow him on Facebook and Instagram @stuart_bray_1991

Also By Stuart Bray

- **The Heretic:** Ren has always been an outcast at his high school. After an invite to a party from the most popular kids in school, his life will take a very dark turn.

- **Every Little Flaw:** Maddison County was once a thriving community, but now, years after the local sawmill shut down, the town is in ruins. The few hold-outs that reside there are too poor to leave. Now, the people of Maddison County must fight to survive the drifters, and a crooked sheriff hell bent on putting the final nail in the town's coffin.

- **Broken Pieces Of June:** June has struggled to find her place in the world. Jumping from town to town, state to state. But when a strange film director shows up and offers her the deal of a life time, a staring roll in her own film... how could she possibly pass it up? only this isn't Hollywood, and though June will be playing a roll... she won't be acting. She will fight for survival in the dark and twisted world of the underground snuff film.

- **White Trash: Broken Pieces Of June II:** Waking up with a massive hole in her gut, June must find the men responsible for the atrocities she faced and take herself from star to director. Lines will be crossed, blood will be spilled, the camera will roll.

- **June: Broken Pieces Of June 3:** In this continuation of White trash: Broken pieces of June 2 the twisted, and depraved "doctors" and "nurses" at the black hill's asylum, are about to meet their new patient. June is back, and she's bringing some old friends along for the ride.

- **Cotton Candy:** Working as a gay male prostitute in 1990's New York, Gavin White has seen it all. That is until he meets a trick that says his name is Mr. Nobody... Mr. Nobody promises Gavin a trip to his own personal "wonderland". Gavin's meaningless life is about to go from bad to worse as he follows Mr. Nobody deeper down the rabbit hole. Cotton candy is a story of love, redemption, and sweet sweet madness.

- **I'll Bury You Tomorrow :** I'll bury you tomorrow features three horrific stories taking place over the span of three different decades. All more gruesome than the last. Will you hear your fortune with Jason on Halloween? will you stay the night at the house of pain in Bateman County? or maybe take a not so pleasant shower in David Birtches penthouse? you decide.

- **Violence On The Meek :** Paul has hated the world and everyone in it since he was eight years old. As an adult he has decided to write his autobiography, his final words directed at the very existence that he despises. Paul will take you on a path of murder, death, incest, and violence, the likes of which you could never imagine.

- **Hillbillies and Homicidal Maniacs (With Jason Nickey):** Stuart Bray joins Jason Nickey (Author of 'Wreckage' and 'Static And Other Stories') to bring you a collection of horror stories. These 6 stories serve as a love letter to old anthologies, but with an Appalachian twist. Jump in on the horror of an infectious glowing orb from the sky, a redneck fight club with a supernatural contender, a cautionary tale of betrayal, a mysterious tape dropped off at a video store, a reflection on childhood trauma, and a brutal tale of revenge.

- **His Name's Vicious :** Vicious is a abnormally large Dutch Shepherd who only wants a stable home... and to rip the throats out of whoever crosses his path.

- **When The Mockingbird Sings (With Jason Nickey):** This is the story of a vile, cruel, disgusting man, getting exactly what he deserves. Johnny is a gangster in 60's Moon City. When Johnny picks up a delivery for his boss at an old warehouse on the edge of town, his life changes in a way you won't soon forget.